Deep Overstock

#13: Future
July 2021

" The future depends on what you do today. "

Mahatma Gandhi

SOC - FUTURE STUDIES

EDITORIAL

EDITORS-IN-CHIEF: Mickey Collins & Robert Eversmann

MANAGING EDITORS: Michael Santiago & Z.B. Wagman

POETRY: Jihye Shin

PROSE: Michael Santiago & Z.B. Wagman

ADDITIONAL COPYEDITING: Vicky Ruan

COVER: Robert Eversmann

CONTACT: editors@deepoverstock.com
deepoverstock.com

On the Shelves

The Prophecy

9 The Pharaoh's Orchid by Amy Van Duzer

10 In the Cards by Karla Linn Merrifield

12 A Future from the Probability Cloud by AJD

18 My Dear Astronomer by John Grey

19 The Price of Getting Old by John Delaney

20 Summit and Depths by Kate Meyer-Currey

21 Dew Point by Kate Wylie

23 Time Trilogy by Timothy Arliss OBrien

The Fall

29 Hyper-Intelligence by Arnold B. Cabdriver

36 Boston, Light the Way by Michael Santiago

43 Blood of the Machine by Bob Selcrosse

53 The Collider by Eric Thralby

The Wasteland

59 Throat Sounds by E.T. Starmann

67 Three Pieces by Ben Crowley

69 Reefless Madness by Nancy Hayes

77 The Student by Eric Thralby

79 God's In His Heaven, And All Orders Will Be Fulfilled by Walter Moon

92 S.A.L. by Bogdan Groza

The Zenith

99 Dear 21st Century by Jonathan van Belle

101 Lost in Space by Karla Linn Merrifield

103 Medicine 2180 by Lynette Esposito

105 Hawthorns by Kate Meyer-Currey

106 The Hymn of Sweet Soul by Yuan Hongri, translated by Yuanbing Zhang

108 Take Refuge in the Sky by Nicholas Yandell

109 Jane, Inc. by K. B. Thomas

113 I Hope by Mickey Collins

Mole drawings by Robert Eversmann

Letter from the Editors

Dearest Readers,

Here we are, in the present, which was once the future, but is just as soon to be the past. When we asked you to send us future pieces you wasted no time in giving predictions, and omens, robots, societies that have crumbled, science gone wrong, science gone weird!

In this issue we tried something new and dare we say futuristic? We've divided the pieces up by theme: The Prophecy, The Fall, The Wasteland, and The Zenith.

"Dear 21st Century," we have here prophecies flown from lighthouse fires, intelligences emerged from growing plastics. We are assembling hopeless wastelands delivered piece-by-piece in Amazon packages. But what's "In the Cards?" A "Time Trilogy," "The Pharaoh's Orchid" and "A Future from the Probability Cloud." You might say we are "Lost in Space," "S.A.L.," high on "Medicine 2180" or "Reefless Madness," or that we are literary drones of "Jane, Inc.," but might "Take Refuge in the Sky." We will tell you reader, we speak to you from the "Dew Point," from futures passed, from "The Hymn of Sweet Soul," from "Summits and Depths." Lend your ear, "My Dear Astronomer," and we will tell you "The Price of Getting Old."

And now we turn from the Future and try our hands at… Magic. Submit your magical piece by August 31st.

Yours, for now and always,

Deep Overstock Editors

THE PROPHECY

Beware the ides of March.

Julius Caesar, 1.2

The Pharaoh's Orchid
by Amy Van Duzer

The Pharaoh, a born idealist but a decided realist, ruled his lands fairly. Although the streets did not shine with gold, the lands were abundant with soil fertile enough for perennial crops of wine grapes, olives, and apricot trees. His people had a dependable harvest in the autumn months, and a large spread on the table each night. The young held hands on their way to school each morning, singing songs of their ancestors before them. The elders never wanted for company, enjoying their family's presence each day.

Every year in the late summer months, the Pharaoh's royal orchid bloomed in different hues, determining news of the year to come. The patriarch and his people waited each year for the flower's color to impress the news upon them. An event was held, and all people attended, waiting to see the fortune of the flower.

All in attendance wore the most recently imported silks with the very best gold jewelry, showing the pure abundance that had blessed their lands and families. Their eyes narrowed as the bud slowly dispersed, showing its petals to the crowd. A scream rang out. The petals outstretched from the bud, shining and black in the late morning sun. The Pharaoh hung his head. It was an omen with a meaning he had never seen before:, an impending death of a royal. With this he turned to his pregnant wife, hesitant to look into her too familiar eyes. The monsoons began that evening.

In the Cards
by Karla Linn Merrifield

The defining moments in our lives often don't come with advance warning. ~ Sally Yates, former US Deputy Attorney General

I read the news today,
then consulted the Tarot.
Seeing myself in the Major Arcana's
High Priestess of unknown secrets
and hidden information, who
dispenses both if I'll listen:
What happens changes a life.
XIII, the Death card,
turns full frontal.

I spend the better
part of a May day
with my better half
at the ER in Rochester,
EMTs expecting
he'd have to be admitted.
Dehydration. Prognosis:
becoming more problematic.
Dementia deep-sixes appetite
for death by starvation;
swallowing reflex shuts down
and he aspirates food,
gets pneumonia, dies.
I know a secret.
I have information.
This is defining.

A Future from the Probability Cloud
by AJD

>The future is a cone, a cone
of possibilities extending
from the present
point.

>The cone
is moving through
space-time, following a
forward arrow, unipolar, directed
towards tomorrow. Our future manifests
out of a cloud of probability from within the cone.

The future is precisely unknown, but looming, a microsecond away, then proceeding into a widening blur of possibility.

This is the dominant image that comes to mind, with hazy origins in some pop physics and cosmology books I read long ago. In some representations, there is a mirrored cone on the other side of the present point, representing the past.

In retrospect, perhaps I am over-scaling the concept of a light cone as a usable metaphor when considering the future, and especially the past. The future is a rumpled blanket of continuity as well.

>The surface
folds, the
fabric threads,
extend from
end to end.

There's a terrain and we're just a small part of it. The context is overwhelming, determinative. The best we can do is try to glean the patterns. We direct our instruments, our imagination, towards this decipherment. Knowledge accumulates, terrain is exploited, the future undermined.

> That's where we are, I think.
> The present point.
>
> Our activities have cast new folds in the blanket.
> We're falling in.
> The threadbare tunnel,
> a scarred battlefield of rapacious extraction, obsessive combustion,
> seems to be twisting into
> a tangled knot of feedback loops and extinctions.

Too pessimistic? On the macro-scale, I might agree. Frogs and bats, though, disappearing by the zillions today, are likely think it too mild a depiction. And I'm with them, and us, because we're next -- and the macro-scale doesn't care.

So, in opposition to what I see as suicidal, ecocidal, business-as-usual, forever-chemical accumulation and profiteering over a cliff, I'll offer a vision of another way -- another future, hopefully better.

I have no special qualifications. I'm no academic, nor even all that well-read. I have some lived experience and a history with lefty media, but nothing that notable. I just feel it is time we, collectively, start articulating these alternative visions more frequently. I offer this essay (with occasional verse) as part of that conversation.

My vision encompasses three overlapping values: universal human rights, equitable distribution of resources, and ecological restoration for future generations. I believe these foundational values, guiding a rationally planned economy, are required to prevent a variety of bad outcomes, from nuclear war to mass starvation.

Humanity reached a certain milestone when, in grave reflection of the smoldering ruins and holocaust of WWII, the newly created United Nations General Assembly of 1948 adopted the Universal Declaration of Human Rights without dissent. Though not yet the force of law, the declaration is similar to the Bill of Rights in the U.S., but adds rights for every person to have healthcare, housing, food, education, freedom from discrimination, and freedom of movement.

These are the rights identified by our forebears to permit a dignified existence to every human being and to prevent the recurring cycles of war and oppression based on want and fear. Putting aside for a moment the mechanism by which such rights might be guaranteed and delivered, the fulfilment of these basic provisions should be an obvious marker to judge a society's success, today and in the future.

As to an equitable distribution of resources, it means what it sounds like: wealth redistribution, from the very rich to the common good.

There are enough resources in the world to provide for both universal human rights and ecological recovery. And there will be in the future, even with the rapid ecological changes and crises we're about to experience. But this basic provisioning is impossible under the current system, where just one percent of the world's population owns half the world's wealth.

A high Gini (inequality) number is not only cruel and arbitrary, it creates its own corrupting feedback loop, as a perpetual machine of lawyers and lobbyists work tirelessly to shovel ever more power and wealth upward, underwriting media and politics to control conversation and regulation. In the United States, where inequality has been growing for several decades, the political system is now plainly oligarchy: that is, legislation inevitably follows rich donors' desires, not voters', as a 2014 study from Northwestern and Stanford showed.

Even many wealthy northern European countries -- long assumed to have locked in human rights such as universal healthcare for their populations -- have seen these rights attacked by the wealth machine's automated functions: corporate neoliberalism, privatization, government austerity. Worldwide, corporations themselves, key instruments in the upward wealth and power funnel, rule over vast empires in tyrannical, dictatorial organization whose sole purpose is to extract ever increasing rates of return to investors, while externalizing common costs.

The process of turning this tide -- of recovering most of the wealth and power wielded by a tiny minority and their legion of representatives, and instead putting it towards the benefit of most people and towards sustaining that which remains of the living planet -- will be a difficult and complex struggle, but it is necessary, arguably more so now than ever before.

This brings me to the third value underlying this vision of an alternative future: ecological restoration for future generations.

We are on the cusp of a human-caused mass extinction event, one featuring cataclysmic events such as drought, widespread flooding, and coastal sea rise which will directly impact billions of people. In an unintended experiment whose consequences are still unclear, we've also doused the entire living biosphere with our chemical pollutants (e.g., PFCs in the Arctic). Further experimentation is underway with the forced introduction and monopolization of genetically modified seeds and organisms -- exciting new markets in the neoliberal regime, on the road to transhumanism for the elite and their guinea pigs.

A lower emission future is feasible, a sustainable system might be installed, the precautionary principle empowered, and humanity's innate values of solidarity and fairness reinvigorated. It can be and should be, if there is to be a better future, as I see it.

The fights are the same. The carbon emissions causing global warming, the toxic pollution contaminating water and critters, the continued offenses in defiance of science and common humanity -- these are an effect of the upward wealth funneling machine. Human-equivalent corporations have captured the regulatory regimes designed to oversee them, and are extracting maximum profit, externalizing the costs of their chemical feast onto and into us. Just as they do with our illness, through a corporatized health industry, and through our lives, through the low-wage, high-rent economy.

So far, I've mostly been committing an offense common to the literature of self-proclaimed alternative vision. I've described the disease and the struggle in some detail, while generalizing the goal of healthy societal alternatives -- specifically, how a better world might manifest and what it might look like. So let me end with some (admittedly kitschy and arbitrary) description of life in an alternative system and the possible paths of transition.

Imagine a movie-trailer voice....

"Imagine a world, where people work by choice, an average of just 12-36 hours a week, producing healthy goods designed to endure or providing skilled services in projects promoting human rights and ecological restoration -- the very tasks required for our collective future. The rest of the time people occupy in activities of their choosing -- largely in personal, familial, cultural, educational, artistic, or spiritual activities. This peaceful, creative, inquisitive, compassionate, and truly productive society might still suffer from many age-old problems, but at least it has a chance to finally transcend the worst brutalities recurrent to their constituents' common history and to build increasingly humane systems in concert with our planet's rich, living ecology."

Such a better world is possible, to borrow from the slogan at the World Social Forum I was once honored to attend. This future world, as I conceive it, could actually be much more productive, despite the scaled back work week, than the current system -- wherein far too much toil remains dedicated towards war, surveillance, the ever-present wealth funneling machine, and manufacturing and distributing disposable goods using increasingly destructive carbon emitting energy.

In opposition to a system which creates excess goods made from toxic materials, within a closed system designed for an infinite growth of excess goods made from toxic materials and toxic waste, it should not be so difficult to articulate a better future and move towards its many possible manifestations. Such a world, with sharing values and wards against structural power accumulation, might soon operate at a far higher level of understanding and progress than we might even be able to imagine today. That's my hope -- and also my excuse for not describing here in further detail my vision for a better future.

As to today's obstructionist political stalemate, and the difficult transformations required to get from here to there, from bad future to better future, I think it necessary to address a conceptual roadblock (often sublimated and subconscious) that often prevents discussions of reform within the working and middle classes that I am most familiar with.

One great fear in the West is that extending human rights and equitably redistributing wealth to everyone will destroy the middle class, or even the working class. If that's your fear, you need to wake up. The middle class today is shrinking by design and, as in robber baron days, becoming skewed towards a specialized high-end coterie of professional and managerial service providers -- at least until, like future Uber drivers, these tasks can be replaced by robots or transhuman handservants.

As for vast spectrum of the working class, in the West and around the world, despite a consistently false and distorted representation to them and about them, for the most part they still know the real enemy is the rich -- and are ready to act accordingly, given the proper provocation.

Which brings us to the current historical moment. As a multi-decade leftist, I've been heartened to see the youth-led activism for environmental and racial justice expressing the need for radical society transformation. Reparations and ecological restoration should go hand-in-hand, especially since it was the exploited and holocausted aboriginal societies which held so much knowledge of the natural systems.

I'll forego the concrete poetry that I started with and just point out that the cone of the past and the future points to here-now, from both directions -- to us. To my magical-thinking mind, this indicates to me that this is the time for us to articulate our better visions for the future. My suspicion is that many will have said it better than this already and my hope is that many more will do so soon. And then, for those of us with the inclination and energy to do so, the work ahead is clear: to make this future materialize out of the probability cloud.

My Dear Astronomer
by John Grey

Don't let an imploding star as seen through
some mega-lens telescope
worry you for our ancient fiery orb.
Your words are measured by
a sputter of hydrogen, the treason of nitrogen,
the unwillingness of breathable air to stick around
when suns give up the flaming ghost.
Your ideas, even on such humble matters as love,
take the gutting of our solar system into consideration,
the fact that every lip you kiss, each cheek you
gently touch with trembling fingers,
is potential space dust, the kisser, toucher, likewise.
Yes, it's all the care they said would never rust
that's now as patchy as a Dalmatian,
the termite-proofed house that's crawling in
those wood-gnawing infidels.
But think of all the good times in that car, that house.
Nothing like a doomed planet
to fire the hormones on all cylinders.
So what if one day there'll be no Shakespeare,
no Kubrick, no elephants, no USA.
Take your nervous eyes off the future for a moment,
reenter the present's atmosphere.
I'm like the sun myself.
What better way of burning out
than burning for you.

The Price of Getting Old
by John Delaney

First, the cost of blood work
and biopsies to analyze
the contents and properties
of your state of ill- or well-being.

The cost of prescription drugs
to regulate your bodily functions
after your deductible or Medicare-
allowable discount or amount.

The cost of physical therapy
to improve the limited motion
of your muscles, joints, and limbs
that succumb to numbing pain.

The cost of X-rays, CAT scans, and MRIs
to determine the sources
and extents of your conditions
for a clearer diagnosis and prognosis.

The cost of open-and-shut surgery
to remove what's not needed,
what part can be replaced,
what went terribly wrong for so long.

The cost of DME (durable
medical equipment), the cane,
the walker, the wheelchair
where you finally commit to sit,

tallying up the hospital bills,
the specialists' invoices,
plan premiums and scheduled payment fees,
swallowing all those pills—

asking how can you now afford it.

Summit and Depths
by Kate Meyer-Currey

I'm riding with the sun to my life's
longest day, one eye to the moon
at my back, drawing me down into
winter's deep waters, where every
year it's harder to rise again to the
surface, weighted by my bones. But
the sun pulls me into buoyant
warmth and I emerge again to its
bright promise, skimming like a
water-boatman over a mirrored
pond, where hope flits like a
dragonfly, for an iridescent moment
as lilies bloom and hungry carp
pout at mayflies and gulp down
their brief day, as dark engulfs
light beneath its inky tide that
recedes as the sun's rays flood
back to melt night's icy rime and
everything dormant under dank
rocks and stones stirs anew with
life, as tadpoles shapeshift into
frogs, mating and croaking at
the sun with rusty winter voices
as the seasons ebb and flow with
the unchanging rhythm of solstice.

Dew Point
by Kate Wylie

At the exact moment where night becomes day,
there's a meet-cute between heat & atmosphere
that only takes place in certain places; not in L.A.
or the Florida Keys, where white-sand minutes
tick strictly forward, but along plainland rivers
where crickets & frogs take turns directing an
orchestra of timber rattlesnakes & cormorants
singing backwards, their wings spread against
stars, sweeping shadows into daylight. We went
at dawn down into the fog-thick valley, just to
listen, our feet dangling from a sycamore
log stretched graciously across the shallow inlet,
blue indigo & purple loosestrife shining in the
almost-morning. I promise, we'll remember this
forever, the way today held out so long, our feet
red with gravel, dipped in the river, cleansed
by moss-thick stones & morning's first glimmer.

Time Trilogy
by Timothy Arliss OBrien

The time trilogy:

1. The past will always stay around to haunt us

1a. Yesterday was the past.
    A monster we cannot move.
      But maybe we can cage it,
Or befriend it.

1b. The past is in the past,
    And now that time has past,
  We can move past,
The past that tries to
  Keep us locked
    in the past.

1c. Don't try to run from the past.
    It has legs and it can move.
It will run alongside you,
    knocking over tables and chairs,
Dictating your future days on past decisions
    without allowing you to control any of the present.

2. Flash forward to present day

2a. Is it really possible to live in the present?
I often feel that the past is ever present
  in my day to day life.
The sidewalks determine my steps,
With cracks that no one can pinpoint
    the day they happened,
But someday long past they became.

The trees grow to give us shade
    from yesteryear's saplings,
      giving us respite from the sun right now,

Today.

The meadowlarks haunt the air
and sing of days past
when they were but warm little eggs
inside the woven little architectures
    of twigs and fuzz in the canopies.

But all I seem to recall of my previous days
    was failure, and an inhibited sense of dread
      that my own history would forever
        hold me back
          and refuse to set me free.

2b. Each present day I try to keep track
    of deadlines and ideas,
        creative lightnings
snaking across my consciousness
    in but a brief mere moment.

I enjoy my time at present walking.
Delving into the lurid concrete jungle
    where each step,
      every second changes the topography
and the social climate of where I happen to be.

I find myself currently with one foot in front of the other,
losing the number of paths I tread
    and hoping if I can lose myself,
      and lose time herself,
        remaining stuck, stagnant, frozen

to the pressures of then, now, and later.

My mornings now mostly consist of sleep
And my insomniatic nights,
    when creativity is not viable,
      are filled with obsessions

about the sordid relationship I hold with the past,

    and the terrorizing agony of fear

that I will disappoint the future.

3. Sometime in the not-so distant future.

3a. How far into the future until we will fully love ourselves? (Asking for a friend...)

3b. "The future is unclear" said the crystal ball to the lady on the other side of the table. But that didn't work for me. I need to know how this will turn out, and this fortune-telling hack and pack of dusty cards will not stop me.

3c. Sometimes we all worry about the future, but worry doesn't change the coming days.

3d. A holy fire burns everything,
In a few days...
   Or years...
     Or decades...
No one knows which generation will feel its purging heat, or how much of God's Green Earth it will eradicate, we can only hope in today, the present.

2c. But what if the present robs us and steals from us the preparation that only the wisdom of yesterday offers?

1d. The past deserves to be left in yesterday.
   Trust me.
Because the future is looming.

3e. But the future is uncertain in all certain terms.

Today is yesterday's future, and tomorrow will be the dreams of today.

And the future is now.

THE FALL

Me miserable! Which way shall I fly
Infinite wrath and infinite despair?
Which way I fly is hell; myself am hell;
And in the lowest deep a lower deep,
Still threat'ning to devour me, opens wide,
To which the hell I suffer seems a heaven.

John Milton, Paradise Lost

Hyper-Intelligence
by Arnold B. Cabdriver

It is hard to tell now what is the absinth and what is the bile. Matyáš and Tomáš contemplate the red doors.

One is the incinerator. One is the future.

The third option, outside, is the plague.

Yesterday, the pods drained of water and two beautiful beings stepped onto the floor.

Father Matyáš.

Father Tomáš.

"Congratulations."

"Success."

So Matyášian plastics had worked. The beings stretched from their pods and shook out their legs. They came and looked through the glass. What had created them? Why were they here?

Matyáš and Tomáš linked arms and danced around the laboratory while the beings watched them through the glass.

"A little absinth for me. A little absinth for you."

That was yesterday. Today was today.

It was not superintelligence, but they were self-learning, self-willed, and beyond our potential by any degree. 'Hyper-,' instead of 'super-,' because these beings had, by every projection, never reached superintelligence, only a far-above-intelligent intelligence, something which was not so much Godlike, as we conceive of the singularity-superintelligence, but something all too human-- unpredictable, unknowable.

'Super-,' the Latin, 'Hyper-,' the Greek, both 'over,' though super, preferred, and hyper, ashamed. The superman. The hyperactive child. The success of Matyáš and Tomáš, admitting they had not achieved superintelligence but "something near close," was met by the Germans with, "Hyperactive-intelligence: leave it to the Czechs to call the singular disorder a success." Hyperintelligence. Matyáš and Tomáš accepted the term. It sounded better than 'suberintelligence.' And Czechs preferred Greek to Latin. The cogito pales in the tall shadows at Delphi.

Matyáš and Tomáš leaned as close as boys to each other over their table, their faces like stones in the eerie green light and the dense smoke around them.

Tomáš worked a bubo between his thumb and forefinger. It poked like a kumquat under his jaw. When finally it broke, it split like the mouth of a can.

"We cannot let her into this world," said Matyáš.

"She is the last of this world," said Tomáš. "She is the only human-thing left."

It gave them each a chill. They each drank again. Each day they knew, was humanity's last.

"She is an abomination," said Matyáš. "She is not humanity."

"She is created in our image. All our hope rests in her," said Tomáš.

The eye of Matyáš drooped under an orb made of skin. He massaged it with his thumbs. A few dribbles dropped to the table. They drank of the absinthe. They glanced at the door. The blond hair inside moved up and down.

"That is not humanity," said Matyáš.

"That is the highest humanity," said Tomáš.

"Can she reproduce?" said Matyáš. "On her own?"

"It's conceivable," said Tomáš. He thought of the man, his blood, his peeled skin, his pubis. "Maybe she already got what she needed from him," said Tomáš. "She could be pregnant right now. Her programming will at least convert what she eats into something which speaks."

"And now that she eats flesh?"

"Well, it is flesh plastics. She will produce a baby much like herself, if she is pregnant."

"And what if she eats organic material?"

"The programming will extract the carbons and begin to form monomer propylene, the rest is waste unless her programming really proves to be self-learning to the extent it produces molecular change at will and even the waste product can be used."

"And what if she eats humans?"

"Humans?!" sputtered Tomáš, his chin buboe squelching from fright. "They are all dead. You've heard the radio. You've seen the TV. It's all static, static, static. Excluding you and me, there are no humans so far as we know."

"So far as we know."

"You're suggesting the possibility of survivors? Look at me," said Matyáš, pointing at his horrible face, a face like a re-animated corpse. "If we are the world's current survivors, what do you expect the others to look like?"

"Imagine if there are survivors, and we unleash this killing machine."

"No, no, no." Tomáš waved him away.

"She is a natural born cannibal," said Matyáš. "The first thing she did out of the pod was eat her mate. They had hardly got the chance to say hello when she bit out her vocal cords. If she does this within the first day of meeting her twin, her equal, what will she do to us ants?"

Tomáš hung his lip. "There is no one left, I assure you. Without us, without her, there would be no chance for humanity. And this is a superior humanity. We have done right. We have done good work. I congratulate you on your Matyášian plastics. And you are too modest. Here you have created new gods and you blame yourself for the end of the world. Here, have a drink. I insist."

Tomáš grabbed the absinth but Matyáš stopped him by the wrist. "She will eat the last of humanity. We have created the Terminator."

Tomáš jerked his wrist away without politeness because Matyáš was acting like a child. "Now I understand," said Tomáš. "You are in a fantasy. You do not understand the nature of this pandemic. We are all dead or dying. It is not my fault. It is not your fault. It is not Honza's fault." Tomáš watched closely as he filled both their drinks. "It simply just is."

"You will let her out of this lab and she will wreak havoc," said Matyáš, seeing the green fill, fill, fill up to the top. "So everyone is dead. OK. She will eat no one alive. But she is capable of reproduction, and might I remind you she is a cannibal in a world made of corpses. If she eats my dead body, your dead body, or any of the hundreds of millions of dead bodies, what will grow inside of her. What kind of humanity will step from her womb? Is that want you want to be known for?"

"Excluding her," said Tomáš. "Who else is there to know us?" He licked and stuck his pinky into the sugar bowl.

Matyáš followed suit and dipped a spoon into the sugar, withdrew it, and lit a match underneath. It burned his hand and bubbled the sugar.

The man and woman were Matyášian plastic. Thermoplastics, like men and women, are carbon-based cellular structures. Plastics are made of repeat units, small carbon-based molecules combined to form monomers, monomers combined to form polymers. For instance, the monomer butene (C_4H_8), the monomer ethylene (C_2H_4), and the monomer propylene (C_3H_6) all contain double bonds between carbon atoms such that the carbon atoms can react to form polymers. True, the monomers (butene, ethylene, propylene) are all sifted through cracking and at no point pre-cracking, cracking, monoization, nor polymerization, do they resemble anything you or I would call life, but, not at subatomic, but only microscopic scale, one may enter Will. All is Fire. All is the Word.

Chemicals are tiny, certainly. But Logos is manipulable infinitely, to any size, to any will, to any material. The matter and the batter. The matter and the matter. Plastic, the mother. Matyáš and Tomáš, the two fathers. They were giddy for it, even in the plague.

At the climax of Matyášian plastics began the end of the world, cousin of the Bubonic plague in the era of the airplane. The two beings in the pods at this time were each the size of a kiwi. Their bodies grew to adulthood, before emerging as two autonomous superintelligences.

Their table shined like an organ.

"Will she burn?" said Matyáš.

"That would be genocide," said Tomáš.

"She has already caused genocide by a half," said Matyáš. Matyáš waved his hand in the smoke, then indicated the door.

They looked over their shoulders

Inside the little window in the red door, the woman's bare legs shined with blood. She sucked his fingers, until she removed the ring finger, which slid red from her mouth. His eyes and his teeth were comically giant because they had no eyelids and no lips.

They turned back to the absinthe.

"Is this really humanity?" said Matyáš.

"Something beyond," said Tomáš.

"If I were smarter, I would eat you. Is this right?" said Matyáš.

"She is not only smart, but more human. She is more human than human," said Tomáš.

"She is pre-singularity," said Matyáš.

"Yes," said Tomáš. "Sadly, we will never reach singularity." He indicated the various buboes hanging from his body. He looked like a child's favorite doll ripped open then restuffed and resewn so many times by the mother that the job was finally given over to the child, and the child had no choice but to plop down and get started, poking anything into the doll within reach, sticking it with the needle again and again, hoping to close it.

"But we have gotten damn close," said Matyáš.

"No, not close," said Tomáš. "It was an emerging intelligence, never an explosion of intelligence. Unfortunately I must say that we have created no God."

Matyáš sighed. He held his hands in his legs, his palms facing up, very simian-like. Matyášian plastics. "Maybe this is the highest desire," he said. "The highest expression. But if the highest desire is the worst of humanity, should we deserve to go on existing? Have we all been cursed to this," he indicated his face, "for some purpose?"

"The exemplar of humanity, the last of humanity, will walk through our cities, birthing and eating her children. Is this your fear?" said Tomáš.

"Orville and Wilbur gave the human race an airplane," said Matyáš.

"Daedalus," began Tomáš.

"Yes," said Matyáš. "Yes, but now we are six billion corpses and only a minotaur."

Tomáš meant to speculate further, but could not for the pain of the lemon, which bubbled from his throat like the sac of a toad.

Matyáš heated a knife under match flame, then pulled Tomáš's face toward him like he was going to give him a shave. Matyáš plugged the knife into the lemon and the lemon coughed.

It does not always matter, the content of your cup.

"Cheers," said Matyáš.

"*-eer-,*" winced Tomáš.

Matyáš and Tomáš grasped hands and shook. Matyáš from the barstool and to the red door of fire. Tomáš from the barstool and to the red door of data. True, 'Matyášian plastics,' he was even inside of the name, but it was Tomáš, Tomáš with his hand on the door, Tomáš opening this door to the new human race. The suction door opened with a gasp and Tomáš held out his hands to their creation. Immediately, her grip looked too tight, but Matyáš could not watch anymore, for the timer on the incinerator had ended and his eyes were quickly eaten by flame.

Boston, Light the Way
by Michael Santiago

A sight upon a site. The hollow beacon stood atop Little Brewster with its majestic gaze. Guiding wayward seafarers from cracking their hull into oblivion. A 12-sided Fresnel lens commanded safe passage to calmer shores, and all at the behest of David Warren, the man who manned this remarkable wonder. He was ordinary, plain in fact, but here he wielded the power of a deity. Without him and his guidance, no vessel would penetrate the dense fog, nor navigate the turbulent tides.

But the price to pay was high. Absolute solitude. Not a soul in sight beyond his guiding light. A job not fit for those who do not enjoy the sound of seagulls, waves, and the innerworkings of their own mind. Only those who can properly care for such a structure can harness its full potential. And only a man who can harness his full potential can care for such a structure. The relationship between man and machine was symbiotic. It had to be. Otherwise, calamity would greet every man astray and reduce any vestige of hope.

This job required absolute adherence every hour of every day. Nothing less would satiate the lightship. This was the order of things, and so it was.

Yet such responsibility can dampen even the strongest will over the course of time. David was no exception to this rule. Four years and counting. No wife, no children, and no next of kin permitted him to take on the mantle.

Outsiders may wonder at how he has been able to subsist on an island with no natural resources, but a dinghy from the harbor would deliver rations and supplies monthly. At times, they would get delivered during the night, and lost at sea by daybreak, succumbing to the tides that rocked the narrow shore.

Life on this rock was routine. Every day was indistinguishable from the last, but today was different. This was the first time David felt something other than himself on the island, but he had no words.

At 2:27 am, he woke to what sounded like the chants of an indigenous man. Flustered, he reached for the gaslit lantern sitting atop the nightstand and shined it throughout the interior of his dwelling. Inching his way outside, the chanting grew louder and louder, and then, nothing. An abrupt silence. The sound of waves and the distant, faint crackle of thunder was all he heard.

An eerie howl emanated from the beacon above, beckoning David to enter the lantern room. This was different from the chanting, but the sense he felt was no different. Something was on this island. Something that should not be there.

He reached for the key to unlock the tower, but the door blew open as he tucked the key in. The lock snapped and the hinge broke due to the velocity of whatever force was inside. Placing each foot in front of the other with caution, he wondered if this was the toll he had to pay for his tenure in isolation. Were his faculties decaying as all things do at sea?

Surmounting each step of the spiral brought him closer to the howl. The chilling sound did not sound welcoming, and intensified as the distance between David and it closed in. Then the chanting returned to accompany the howl. He raised his lantern forward with a widened gaze. Spooked and covered in goosebumps, he hesitated to move forward, yet he had to. He had to protect the very construct that was designed to protect.

The crisscross of scratching began to resound within the concave. Howls, chanting, and now scratching. He bellowed out with only a few steps left, and again, abrupt silence.

Letting out a slight sigh of relief, he muttered, "Who, if anyone, is there?"

Before he could raise his lantern into the chamber, he was thrust against the wall. Slamming his head against the Fresnel lens. The light dimmed and grew faint as he began to lose focus and shut his eyes.

Engulfed in a sea of silence, he was alone inside the hollow shell.

Clasping each hand onto the ground, he pushed himself up and opened his eyes to see a scorched city before him. The sounds that echoed within the lighthouse were replaced with piercing screams. They grew louder and louder. Sirens whistled down the adjacent streets. Children cried from buildings set ablaze.

Boston was crumbling. Fire danced from one obstruction to the next. It gorged on anything impeding its path. A grisly spectacle unlike anything the city had seen before. Looking on in horror, David could not rationalize what he saw.

He shook his head frantically as if trying to awaken from a dream, but this was as real as any other moment in his life. Unsure of what to make of it, he began running as buildings collapsed and structures disintegrated. Plumes of smoke ruminated throughout the city as the harsh orange glow lit up the sky. Seagulls plummeted from the sky as toxins infiltrated their lungs.

A few meters away, a stray dog was nursing her offspring outside of an apothecary that was ready to topple. Sprinting to try and remove the dogs from impending doom, the roof smashed down onto their position. Their howling and cries ceased.

In a parallel building, a family of three were trying to flee using a fire escape until it rattled and tossed them onto the ground with the structure falling on top. In the distance, he could see two others trapped within a burning building with no way to escape. Screams and cries for help echoed across the city. Charred bodies fell from the surrounding structures as the unrelenting fire consumed.

This chaos could not be doused. It continued rippling across the city as it satiated its desire to feed. In a panic, David stopped and looked around him shouting, "how is this happening?"

"It's yet to happen," a voice bellowed within.

"Who is talking?" he replied.

Slamming his fists against his forehead, he uncontrollably screamed. Suddenly, the sound of sirens halted, the blistering heat subsided, and the scent of smoke receded. He opened his eyes and realized he was lying on the floor next to the shattered Fresnel lens. As his line of sight shifted, he jumped up and fell back. Four indigenous shamans stood before him. They glared at him with an indescribable intensity. David began convulsing as a result of his panic-stricken state.

"Who, who are you?" he quavered.

"You ask too many questions," said the first shaman.

"So, you can speak English?" he mumbled.

"Again. Questions. We speak what you understand," said the second shaman.

"Just as you saw, the city will burn," a third shaman said.

The fourth shaman, much larger in stature, slammed a large wooden staff onto the ground to quell the others' commotion. His face was a canvas for a blood encrusted crimson skull. A wolf hide adorned his head and beads were tethered around his neck and arms. Strange ancient symbols carved into his chest began to glow a pale blue hue.

Pacing towards David, he orated, "Two generations ago, this land was ours. All of it. Even where you stand now. As you and your people came, our lives and our land were stolen from us. Many of us offered peace, but you were the harbingers of death. And for us, those imbued with otherworldly gifts, we were forced to this rock to be executed. Without the right of passage to the next world, we remained."

With a momentary pause, the other three shamans began to chant and dance counterclockwise within the chamber. Once more, the large shaman spoke, "What you saw will happen. We have channeled what you may refer to as precognition. Foreseers of what will come and what will ever be. You have been offered a glimpse of the catastrophe that will destroy your settlement across the sea. We are not vengeful spirits. We still offer peace in exchange for our deliverance, but we cannot stop what is to come. This land has enough blood soaked in the soil."

"What could a humble keeper of this busted beacon do?" David questioned.

"The method and means are not up to us. We have merely made ourselves known to offer you a glimpse into the future," the large shaman replied.

"When will the inferno arrive?" he asked.

"By daylight, but this is one of many possible futures," the shaman stated.

With those last cryptic words, the four-shaman chanted and howled and continued to dance in a circle. It resonated across the whole island until the figures began to fade and the voices slowly silenced.

Again, he was alone.

Still stirred, a dumbfounded look plastered his face. He had to surmise that this future was the inevitable outcome that these lost spirits foretold. That Boston would be met with a future full of fire and brimstone.

Glancing at the shattered crystal orb in the center, he figured the only way he could help was to send a signal through the towering granite sentinel. Yet, the glass dome that refracted light to the vast sea was cracked, and the only replacement could be found in the city, several miles away.

"Colloid," he gleefully declared.

Never expecting to use the colloid gel, it eluded him during many occasions where its use was warranted, but it was the only means of repairing anything on Little Brewster. Strong enough to hold the fragments together and retardant enough to endure the heated dome. At least for a short while. Nonetheless, he sprinted down the concave spiral and back to his dwelling. Rummaging through every drawer until he found it.

Alas, the gel was tucked away in the utensil drawer in the kitchen, and with haste, he made his way back to the top of the beacon. Frantically grabbing each fragment, with trembling hands, he began gluing the lens as close to its initial state as possible. With the lens holding in place for now, he twisted the bulb and stood back.

However, the bastion of light did not immediately turn on. In a bewildered state, David extended a brass spy class to peer across the shore. Wondering where he could send the signal, he spotted a fire station across the road from a stable. He knew that that would be the location to shine the beam. Even if the fire started, the fire fighters would at least be awake to respond. That this vision of the future could be skewed if the conditions were altered.

Then, without notice, the crackle of sparks within the dome strobed the light for a few seconds. This continued until the light became a solid beam, reflected through the interior of the lens.

"The station. That is the only way," he thought.

Grasping the iron spindle, he began rotating the focus of the beam to the estimated coordinates. As the light shot across the sea, it radiated within the adjacent stable; a few degrees off his intention. Within the stable, several trained fire horses were sleeping. Weakened by the effects of a flu, the horses grew restless by the overbearing ray of light.

A few of the horses kicked and wrestled with the blinding beam. One of the horses bucked and catapulted a hail bail towards a gaslit lantern. Knocking it over, the combustion gobbled up the hay and set the entire stable ablaze. The cries of stallions rattled within as the bonfire fed.

At this hour, hardly anyone was awake. David looked on

gasping in horror. He watched from his spy glass as the flame cascaded from the stable to the nearby buildings. Scorching everything that crossed paths with the untamed flame. Dancing across rooftops; leveling block after block. David turned around and slid his back down the side of the interior. Dread and defeat blanketed him.

"Years spent protecting these shores, yet an inferno in the horizon grew hungrier by the second," he said. This was the vision. Manifested by his own hand.

Blood of the Machine
by Bob Selcrosse

There was no delay in my work. The lathe machines were pumping. I could not get them to stop, no matter how much I begged them. There had never been such demand.

The machines of our street pumped into the night. The air above the tarmac was a shimmering metal dust. As the sun angled down at night, the light twisted over the dust like a loose pack of ribbons. We squinted and breathed through towels we held over our lips.

You may recall that the Great Zelazny had taken our elderly and flown into the sky. We had no choice but machines. And I, a poor lathe man, was making parts to things I'd never dreamed of--mechanical legs to a mechanical armchair on which men could relax. Pull the lever and the footboard popped up your feet. I made the hinges in the door of a mechanical washing machine. It rattled there while the user turned it on. My neighbor and I filled it with water and soap. He threw his children's clothes inside it and we went for a beer. When we returned, his garage was spilled edge to edge with soapy water which curved into the street like a tail, snatching up metal filings like collecting confetti. My neighbor pulled out the clothes--they were as white as new teeth.

I want to preface this before I say to you, I did, on occasion, overworked and underpaid, create pieces to things I consider morally unconscionable. But then I am only the maker of parts. A nut is a nut. A bolt is a bolt.

But then I saw the horrible fruits of my labor. My neighbor invited me again to the unveiling. Only this time it was not a clothes washing machine. The figure lay on the floor. It had two arms. It had two legs.

My neighbor handed me a small box with an antenna and a large red button. The red button. The figure on the concrete garage floor stood up by itself. It turned its head back and forth. It was unsteady on its feet, stepping, misstepping, correcting. It stood up to a hunch, drooping its arms. Its shoulders jerked back and then forth until finally it came to stand upright, as straight as me or my neighbor.

Its gaze was so intense. My eyes in response opened too wide, as if they would never stop opening. It felt like jumping into a hole, but I looked away and focused on my neighbor's thirty drawer tool box. I pressed again the red button. The standing thing, as if under the relief of miniature hydraulic pumps, jerked section by section as it gradually collapsed to a heap on the floor. Its eyes did not close. It had no eyelids. It continued to stare from the floor.

The next morning I clicked on the lathe and it whirred into life. It was then I heard the children.

They were playing with a can, kicking it idly, then kicking it violently, a very strange can, kicking it, striking it on the pavement, just as boys would. Perhaps they were friends of the great boy detective.

The can rolled up to my feet. Surely, I should hand it to one of them, dress them down, tell them not to kick trash up-

I kicked it.

The boys chased after it, then they kicked the can suddenly into the garage of a neighboring machinist. I felt like a boy again. How good it was to play. How refreshing. The can echoed in the garage, then rattled to a still. The boys did however not pursue the can any further. In three, two, one--my neighbor's garage exploded.

Investigators arrived in yellow jackets and their hands on their hips. The garage still plumed black arms of dust. Finally,

an investigator, one hand with a flashlight, and the other holding the lip of the entrance, stepped into the smoke. Three investigators followed him. They disappeared completely.

My neighbor was a widower. Shaken but unharmed, he held a red sheet over his shoulders and sipped a paper cup.

The shoulders of the investigators emerged. They dragged out a metal tangle. It scraped high-pitched against the street. A pile of legs and of arms, the twisting black metal like beams reaching up in a fire, as if they were growing.

The investigators all let go at once and the pile rocked like an extremely heavy washer. The head was glued to the shoulder. The arms were glued to the legs. The eyes were invisible, but I felt them peeking out from an elbow. Altogether, it looked like a smelter down on his luck had needed to melt down his favorite metal sculpture for food money, but killed the blast furnace at the last minute.

An investigator handed my neighbor the little box. It two was burned and partially flattened by heat. He brushed off the button, then pressed it. The head turned in the pile. My neighbor's own head dropped and his shoulders began to pulse. He had lost everything. Everything was gone in the fire--his lathe, his father's lathe. There was nothing left but a gaping black hole.

I put a nickel into the machine under the streetlight so thick with crawling ivy it seemed to droop toward the street. I dialed for the great boy detective.

"You have dialed-"

"Fuck," I said. I threw the phone back on the hook and gave it a second nickel.

"Hello," said the great boy detective.

"There's a dead man," I said.

"I know," he said. "How do you know?"

I looked through the glass. A tow truck driver had his finger on a button lowering his tow-gate. "I'm looking right at it," I said. The pile of robot was already on a hook and chain, the tow arm out and the fronalready hovering one end of it slightly off the ground.

"That's funny," said the great boy detective. "So am I."

I looked around more frantically this time. No, he was nowhere.

"Come to the wet market," he said.

Busy signal.

"Your call cannot be completed-"

"Fuck," I said. I hurled the phone to its cradle.

The great boy detective had a six pack of those wax bottles with red or blue flat soda where you twisted off the top and it left candley residue all day on your fingers. He had just finished one and tossed his empty back into the cardboard tray, then withdrew two red ones so we matched. He twisted the tops and looked on at the body. Three investigators were all squatted around it. They were, I thought somewhat inappropriately, poking and prodding it with various medical-looking instruments, one with a q-tip and a handful of tiny plastic baggies, one with massive metal tweezers, and the third with his own blue-gloved fingers. The man was in a pile of blood, therefore he was not a robot.

"Time of death?" I said.

"Seven-thirty this morning," said the great boy detective. "Yours?"

"Seven-ten, seven-fifteen," I said. "Think they're linked?"

He pointed at the body beside an investigator's foot. A small yellow fold-card with the number "1," and beside it a little metal box with a red button and antenna.

"I see," I said. I drank my flat soda. It was like kissing candy lips. How did he always know what I was up to? How was he always one step ahead?

"Your neighbor was involved in something," said the great boy detective. "Your whole street, I suspect. You've been making unfamiliar parts."

"Yes," I said. "And they're being put in unfamiliar things."

There were a few shady characters, denizens of the wet market, wringing the brims of baseball caps or dirty aprons, looking on at the dead man. For a brief moment the tallest one, a grizzled and burly old bald man with a great beard of black, I thought, The Great Zelazny. But no. This man's eyes were too dead, too yellow. He was just some other bastard beard.

An investigator approached us with his hand behind his back. The other investigators watched us from the body. "I thought you might want this," said the investigator. He produced a floating yellow balloon tied to a silver string and handed it to the great boy detective, saying, "Thanks for all your special help in this investigation." Though his face turned crimson and he gritted his teeth, the great boy detective accepted the balloon and used 'sir' when he thanked him. The investigator sneered.

The boardwalk had become more and more popular in recent weeks. Maybe the spell of good weather, or the discounted mangoes, or just the disappearance of the old--whatever it was, the boardwalk had for the first time in years a striking lack of dread and an overall sense of uncomplicated delight. But we were on business. The great boy detective set his wax sodas by a red and yellow ticket booth. The man inside, smoking a cigar that resembled a finger and produced faintly green toe-smelling smoke, shoved open the window of his ticket booth and stared at the balloon.

"You're too goddamned short," he said. He pointed at a You-Must-Be-This-Tall measuring sign red and yellow to match his booth. This, for the recently refurbished wooden roller coaster we all knew as "The Rat."

"We're here on business," said the great boy detective.

The man coaxed a long string of spit from his mouth to the boardwalk boards, some of which passed through to the ocean. He slurped up the lingering strand and wiped his grizzled face before pushing his window even wider. "Is that right?" he said.

The great boy detective stood on his toes and slipped a ten-dollar bill on the booth's counter. The man, who I now saw was as stained and wrinkled as a palm tree, snatched up ten as if it were a bug. All pretenses off, the man stepped out of his booth and the great boy detective absently left his wax sodas and let his balloon fly away.

"Follow me," said the man. He hiked up his pants. He wore a belt and suspenders. He walked not unlike a cartoon. He took us down the boardwalk, behind the coaster and to a wooden set of stairs down to the beach. We creaked down, they jostled side to side every step, as if they were suspended on strings. Underneath the shade of the boardwalk, there were a group of children being cradled by machines.

The man chewed the butt of his cigar and held up his palm. The great boy detective just looked at it. I shoved into my own pockets and gave the man a ten.

"Five minutes," he said. He exhaled like a man who loathed exercise, then returned up the stairs. Wooden dust floated from the boards as he departed along the boardwalk back to his booth.

We approached the machines. They were like the cars or helicopters outside of grocery stores that you sat in and jostled you if you gave them a quarter. Only they were flesh-colored and old, many of them wore robes, all of them spectacles, and many of them, squatting there cradling the children, had swollen ankles, fleshy and popping with varicose veins icy blue under the dark of the boardwalk. The children in the machines watched us. They were not idly cradled. Some turned over on their stomachs and peeked under the elbows, holding their fingers on the fingers of the machines.

"I don't like this," I said.

"Nor do I," said the great boy detective.

They were of all ages, some very young, some even older than the great boy detective.

"How do you know about this?" I said.

He shrugged. "I keep my ear to the ground."

"It's creepy," I said.

A boy, cradled in the sagging arms of a rather fat machine, glowered at me. He seemed not calmed at all by his ride on the machine, but ready to spit a big one in my face. The machine began patting his hair and the boy closed his eyes. The machine wore a medical bracelet and many tarnished turquoise rings.

"They are here to fill the void I suppose," said the great boy detective. "The void since the circus."

The circus takes everything away.

"Hold on," said the great boy detective. He held his arm out stopping me. "What's that?"

I scanned up ahead. There was nothing but the myriad of machines and all the near-catatonic children. But then, in the back, obscured almost completely in shadow, there was a boy standing up. He stood tall and hastily pulled on a jacket.

"Hey," said the great boy detective.

The shadow bolted.

We ran for him through the dark under the boardwalk. The light was only stripes. We chased him lunging through

Blood of the Machine

the sand, though he was so fast he only got further and further away. Finally we came to a second set of wooden stairs. We knew from the sound he'd leapt up them, so we followed suit. By the time we were back on the boardwalk, it was only our guess as to which direction he went. We headed in the direction of the Ferris wheel, then heard a scream behind us.

The great boy detective stopped in his tracks. "The ticket man," he said.

By the time we'd got to the booth, it was already too late.

The booth was so narrow that the ticket man did not lie but sat upright in a pool of his own blood, his right arm straight up, the heel of his palm still hooked on the counter. His white eyes were wide open in terror and he had partially swallowed his cigar so only the embers stuck out, still smoking, and burning his lips. In the left center of his chest where his heart should have been, there was an enormous bloody hole, the suspender strap hovering over it, not unlike the crude string of a one-string guitar. Bloody footprints led away from the ticket booth to the carnival games. We followed.

Red and white party lights criss crossed over the corridor of games. Most were abandoned, shuttered stands or dark pits with rats licking the milk bottles or sleeping in the abandoned stuffed animals. But inside one in every three stands, there was still a carny ready to fleece you with fifty coke bottles and a heavy glass ring.

"Step right up," said a carny, tossing a resewn softball up and down. "Step right up."

The great boy detective confronted the carnie with his hands out like he would choke him.

The carny stepped back. "Wo," he said.

"We're looking for a man," said the great boy detective.

"A man?" I said, taken aback. All this time I thought it was a boy.

"Yes, a man," said the great boy detective. "You're going to tell me now if you've seen someone come through here."

What the carnie said was fairly hard to understand. When we squinted, he pointed. There were four bloody fingerprints on the outer-edge lip of one stand.

"Do you have your firearm?" said the great boy detective.

"Uh-huh," I said. I drew my gun and we walked steadily forward.

A collection of sounds grew as we approached the stand, something like the inner workings of a mouth, the slapping and gnashing of teeth and a tongue, but also something mechanical, something like the top bobbin of a sewing machine, the thin metal fingers that drew its thread into the needle of the machine. We walked toward the back of the stand. Whatever it was doing, it was doing it behind the games stand.

"I have a gun," I said. We had only one step, one step and we would be around the corner and facing the murderer. "I have a gun," I said slowly. We turned the corner.

There was the man. His eyes were as clear and confused as the eyes in a retirement center. His mouth, chin and fingers were drenched completely in blood and still dripping. He was shoving the last pieces of something in through his teeth. The expression in his face meant only, I have no idea what I'm doing.

His jacket had fallen partially open and I could see inside a hint of what whirring process was making the sounds of a bobbin. That area too had a concentration of blood. As I approached him, he made no move. He had swallowed the last of whatever he'd had in his fingers, and now kept his hands down stiffly beside his legs as he sat, dazed and breathing heavily.

With one hand, I held my gun steady. Then with my other I reached in and parted his jacket. His insides were silver and in his chest, a dozen bobbin fingers pulsed in and out of a red bulging material as more red matter fell through the gears in his throat and through the working parts to join the organ in his chest. The shiny pulsing fingers had recomposed the heart, which was now beginning to beat. I closed the jacket.

The man could not remember his name, nor if he had had a name, nor whom he had served, nor whom he had grown up with. The family he had served arrived to claim him. Two young children hugged his varicose legs. The mother produced a small silver box from her purse. When she pressed the red button, the heart inside stopped beating, and the old man collapsed in a heap.

"Another case closed," I said.

We celebrated on the boardwalk with two banana splits with Neapolitan ice cream, crushed pistachio nuts, hot fudge and whipped cream dollops.

The great boy detective stared wistfully out at sea. "Again, we have run our emotions too freely," he said. Fluffy clouds passed over like a graze-land's lazy sheep. "This is what the circus should teach us." He pressed his ice cream around with his spoon. "There is a limit and we must keep that limit at all costs. Never cross over that limit. Never cross over that limit. Never cross over that limit."

It occurred to me then that the murderous robot had had the face of his grandfather, the great boy detective's wise old grandfather. Then I too looked in the sky. Why must you do this to the great boy detective? The clouds became misty and frightened.

The Collider
by Eric Thralby

Our town's favorite men were the men in blue jumpsuits who walked into the forest then down into the collider. The collider was a good way's underground. It went under the forest, then under our town. We prayed for life to our collider, on our knees beside our beds. Our bed stand waters rippled as it whirred. The collider would give us something alright.

The first major change occurred outside the Old Thorn Retirement Home. It was a fear which crept through the residents like rumor or a virus. It had them up at night with their covers coming up to their nose and the toes of their grippy socks exposed. Residents called the staff on their emergency buttons. They would point from their beds with their tired old fingers. *The tree. That tree. The tree.* Only the west-facing residents, having west-facing windows, windows facing the sycamore tree. It had grown a pair of eyes. No orderly believed this. In fact, the residence was running out of drugs due to its west-window having patients. Even through their cottony blinds they were sure they saw the tree blinking. The orderlies merely fluffed up their pillows and stuck their arms full of opium.

The next major change was more inexplicable, more undeniable, more unavoidable. The north- and south-facing windows at the Arms Apartments had sprouted threads overnight, as if hundreds of spiders had all jumped to their deaths and were carried on by the wind. North- and south-facing residents, poking their heads from their windows, found their neighbors were no different, that was, at least the neighbors between the first and fourth floors. The second floor and the fourth floor. Every window, a dozen gossamer strands each, some up to ten-feet in length bound up by the breeze. They swept the strands in their fingers and flicked with their hand out the window until they all unstuck and flew off. But of course the next morning, the strands were back, ten-twenty percent thicker, more like strands of hairs, stuck to their windowsills and reaching to the ground. Eventually, they grew like vines. You could prune them off with shears, but they would be back by morning just as thick. You could stay up all night and prune every ten minutes, but how many nights could you stay up in a row? The vines grew so thick that children could slide down them to the ground. Though fun for some, they were disturbing to many, for the vines were flesh-colored and seemed to grow veins. A year of this and the vines grew so entangled and thick they were as strong as two trees, enormous trees, which bent as if elbowed from the windows to the ground. In the middle of the night one night, the Arms Apartments rocked to life. Books flew from the tables and dishes vomited from the cupboards. Residents, stepping over their floors as it quaked, rushed to their windows to see their apartment complex leave the ground and start walking, two massive flesh-colored branches, eerie in the night, stepping forward rhythmically, as if the apartment were a man without legs, stepping palm by palm down the street. It walked this way for weeks until it got to Labrador where it came to a stop, set the apartment upright near a sea cliff. There it stayed for six months, where everyday residents enjoyed the seabirds of the ocean and the violent crashing waves.

Everywhere flesh swelled in our buildings. We put our hands to our faces and wondered, what was this? What had we done? Anyone of us might catch our toe on a vein and stagger into the living room, or everyday slip our hands through thin skin, peel it apart and pin it in place for the day, just to see out the window. It had not happened to me, but I know some friends who've been licked. A young heartbroken woman, as if mocked by an alien fate, went mad with her ear to her wall every night, listening, listening to the beating heart growing inside the other apartment.

Our friends in blue jumpsuits came up from the underground collider to ask questions. They put their instruments into the skin, what appeared to be the heel of a foot, first a thermometer, then a listening device, and then they drew blood. It was not human, they knew that much. It was, in fact, no flesh of this earth! Except now, of course, it was everywhere. It was some race of enormous, inexplicable, extra-dimensional beings.

There is only one man who can save us. He is stalky, a little fat, and wears an orange jumpsuit. His hair is short and black, a little wild, and everyday he wears glasses. He wears the Doc Martin boots which, more like shoes, do not cover the ankle and, inside those, mismatched pink and purple socks. He does not know his old name. Because he was stolen as a baby. Everybody now just calls him 'The Body.'

THE WASTELAND

The earth will tremble and writhe in agony. For the Lord will carry out his plan. He plans to make the land of Babylonia a wasteland where no one lives.

Jeremiah 51:29

Throat Sounds
by E.T. Starmann

We needed only six gestures.

Why would you need more?

They are made with the body. The mover may lie, sit or stand, though the meaning may change. They are not written down. I have written them for your convenience, reader.

How do you use them?
As I am the tower guard, I might say:

a. : 'open the gate'

b. : 'one, approaching the gate, identified, uninjured, unaccompanied'

c. : 'unknown number, approaching the gate, unidentified, uninjured'

Why do you use them?
As I am the tower guard, the actions of the gate man follow. That is, the gate man, having looked up and received my gesture, will, correspondingly:

a. : the gate opens, gate man sends for no doctors

b. : gate man sends for armed accompaniment, not for doctors

c. : community emergency

Appropriate scenarios are met with appropriate responses.

Take, for example, the event : 🯅

    'one approaching gate, unidentified, injured'

In this event, armed accompaniment will arrive at the gate to support the gate man as the gate man opens the gate. Doctors will be called for.

Never was 🯅 mistaken for 🯅 , nor 🯅 for 🯅 .

Never has 'one approaching gate' been confused with 'no one approaching the gate.' Never has 'injured' been met without adequate medicine.

Do not doctors need mouths?
Do not doctors need books?

I will direct your attention, reader, from the tower to the ground. See now the man in the dirt. His leg is bent in half. He is holding his knee. See the anguish in his face, how quiet he is. See now, three generations of medicine:
    the master with the cultus
    the mentor with the bowl
    the intern like a shadow
A knife squeezes into the skin. Everything is said in this way. Patient to physician, eye to eye, all through the surgery, a long cold stare.

I am perpetually above everyone else, so they have turned me into a joke.

    🯅 🯅 🯅   :   'bird man'

I find eggs in my tower—chicken eggs, robin eggs, duck eggs, sometimes with a nest. I have never sired a child. I am doubly a joke.

 : 'without child'

There is an impenetrable white cloud outside the gate. From what lurks inside, I keep the community safe.

My sister is wife to the gate man. The gate man is a dolt.
He forever complains of his neck. *How sore I make his neck.* He is forever rubbing, glaring, waiting for my word.

🯅🯅🯅 : 'invasion'

🯅🯅🯅 : 'return'

I am the crick in his neck. He is the prick in my sister. I have no one. I have literally no one.

🯅

The cloud did not pass through our bodies but pressed from the sky, an immense climatological pressure squatting down to our chests on its haunches, a dwarf on the breast of our sleep.
At times, the cloud clambers over the gates, and I am lost in my tower, a punt adrift in a white, wide ocean.
The cloud took language. How could it be otherwise? See how thickly it circles, like hills to a valley, or a circling mountain, so enormous and white, like a white anaconda filling our canyons.

I have dreamt every night of a child. For who will keep watch when I'm dead?

One night the wall was impenetrably thick.

I to my brother-in-law : 🯅 🯅

Throat Sounds

I don't give a goddamn about clouds! You're killing my neck! —his gestures too informal to write. He continued flirting with the moonherd's daughter.

But I knew something was out there. I toed to the edge of the tower. What was it? It appeared as a stone does in wheat. A trout in the rapids. A moon stepping out through the clouds.

'one approaching the gate, unaccompanied' :

'unidentified' :

'possibly injured' :

, I gestured like a gunshot.

The gate man caught me and put his hands on the gate. We do not often open the gate. It is the most immense thing we do. When the gate opens, the community quakes.
The cloud toed in like ghosts from a mist. Community members shivered. All watched. I barred down from the tower.

In the cloud—a tiny boy.

The boy was deformed. His ears were lumpy and he did not have proper teeth. His throat was scarred. Hair did not grow evenly from his head. Where had he come from? What threat could he be? I bundled him up. I held his throat to my ear. Something was inside, making noise of its own.

I took him first to the doctors. The middle doctor dumped red clear realgar in two thin plastic cups meant for pills, one for me and one for him, we made a mess on the counter. He sweated and was watched by the superior doctor. All three listened to the baby's throat. It was a gurgle. It was a vibration. But it could be removed. We arranged it for morning. For now, the middle doctor tied a towel over its mouth, which seemed more to soothe than disturb. The superior doctor tugged greedily of the realgar, as the intern read his pulse through his fingers.

I took him next to the mothers. I hoped for their gestures. Two I knew isolated as 'one approaching the gate, unidentified, injured, unaccompanied,' and 'one approaching the gate, identified, uninjured, unaccompanied,' however in quick succession:

I learned meant 'ugly,' 'ugly.' For at this time the throat's babbling was audible even under the towel. At the shock of what was happening around me, at having a baby, at hearing its sound, at the women's rejection, I opened my mouth. As this was a sexual organ, the tent flap was pulled up and it was indicated I leave.

Ashamed, I took the baby to the tower. It was beginning to rain. In this future, above which we are flattened by clouds, rain leaves white streaks of mist like hot wisps of smoke. I climbed into the tower alone where the baby could not be seen, could not be heard.

I routinely gestured this to the baby. 'Good baby.' 'Good baby.'

The baby made a sound, which I remembered as 'ah.'

Then lying started.

I watched from the tower. The gate man beat his children. He boxed them on the ears. After little girls had heard the baby 'da' and 'ba,' they had found themselves finally the two-letter word 'no.'

 : 'did you climb over the gate?'

I watched the gate man. I watched my nephews. They did not respond in a way their father understood. They did not move their bodies. Their legs and arms remained still. They opened their mouths and merely said, 'no.'

It was as if everyday the cloud tightened.

Tradition that community elders strained themselves before death. Reaching sixty, even seventy, they pulled the sheets quickly back down from over their heads and, straining their throats so they swelled and their faces turned red, they tried to utter last words. But now, as the children learned 'no,' 'yes,' 'goodbye,' the elderly strained into these fugue states as early as forty or fifty. In their beds, they grit their teeth so intensely, but still nothing came out. It was only just before death some finally gasped '*uh*' like a flat puff of air.
Fat white tails lifted from the chimneys of our crematoriums and crept, as if finger by finger, into the overhung cloud.

'I'm sorry,' 'Forgive me,' the children were learning so quickly. Children do not care as to the state of the world until it has reached in to hurt them.

Someone left a dead baby bird in my tower:

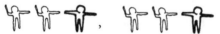

I taught my baby key defense gestures:

The destruction of a community is dealt with by medical professionals. As the master physician had perished, we had only the apprentice and shadow.

'I think of you as the right man for my sister,' I said.
He flicked an injection needled then pumped it so it tossed a sharp line of liquid into the air.
'Is this the operation you were meant to do on my baby?' I said.
'I never learned that operation,' he said.
He jammed the needle into my mouth. It was like a mosquito, only it was not taking my blood, but putting its blood in me.
'What is this?' I said.
'Numbing agent,' he said.
My mouth became cold.
'My apprentice can do nothing,' he said. 'Look at him.'
He indicated the shadow who, across the room, was spilling and fixing metal trays of cotton balls, tongue depressors, small iodine bottles. Everything he fixed fell to the floor again. It was as if a table's legs had collapsed and he was the only thing holding it up. He could not let the goods fall, and he could not let the table fall, and so all things perpetually fell.
'I have used words,' said the doctor. 'I have said only three objects: speculum, cultus, stethoscope. And look at the mess I am in.'
Tinny bowls clattered from cupboard to shadow and the boy waved at bandages, as if they were moths.
The doctor gathered a long black thread, like what might be used to sew up a football, and tied it through the eye of a needle.
My tongue recoiled when the needle first popped through my mouth. He worked his fingers and reappeared the needle before my eyes, grimy with my skin and my blood.
I reached to my mouth. The black thread crisscrossed my lips like the legs of a Harlequin. The doctor put my hands in my lap.
In moments, I was unable to speak.

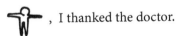 , I thanked the doctor.

Three Pieces
by Ben Crowley

The Light Tower

There is an immense light on immense legs. It is as if the bulb of a lighthouse were rolled onto the legs of a water tower. As men lose their hair and graduate high school, they ascend the ladder up the tower. They got a woman pregnant, or had to shave their head, or lost a testicle to cancer. They sling beers down their backs and climb up the light. At 1,000 Watts, a Tungsten bulb burns at 575 degrees. They drink beer until they can push themselves into the light.

The Mounted Speaker

There is a mounted wall speaker which the men gather, too.

You are hateful, says the mounted wall speaker.

The men push their heads closer to the concrete wall under the speaker, as if they were piglets pushing for the nipples of the sow.

You are dirty tricksters and liars, says the mounted wall speaker.

The men push so hard that some chests collapse and the bodies of the dead men dangle, suspended in the sea of ravaging shoulders.

You are rotten eggs, says the mounted wall speaker.

The Television

The man comes into the television room.

I have had enough of this life, says the man to the television.

The television shows the man an ad for Pepsi-Cola.

I said I have had enough! says the man.

The ad for the Pepsi-Cola becomes louder than the man can think.

Enough! says the man.

The apartment fills with the refreshing scraping and clacking of a thousand cans of Pepsi-Cola.

The man crawls to his television, reaching out to it, as if it will pull him from the crevice of living. *Pepsi. Cola,* he says.

The television spits on the man. It reminds him of his mother.

Reefless Madness
by Nancy Hayes

Secret aaaagent man--
A tee.
Secret aaaaagent man--
A tee.
They've given you some blubber
And taken away your mane.
   --Johnny Estuaries

From his waterfront office, located within the mangroves and womangroves of Kissimmeeyoufool, Florida, Secret Agent Manatee logged into his laptop. A new episode of his favorite whalepodcast, *Last Night Spumes Raydio* had been posted to Deep Overboard's website. In this episode, spumeists Flukey Collins, Blubby Eversmann, Brine Sprinkle and Toonah Collins would create shrimprovised flash-poems based on the night's special theme, "The Past." Since the listening audience was encouraged to play along, Secret Agent Manatee grabbed a sea pen, a bottle of squid ink, a piece of sandpaper and a glass of Reefsling and awaited instructions.

"In the first of tonight's three rounds, your task is to write a spume evoking old-timey times--using only future tense verbs--in the form of a *tanka*, a thirty-one-syllable poem, traditionally written in a single unbroken line," announced Blubby. "Fellow spumeists, you have five minutes to write your tankas, tanka you very much. Flukey?"

Flukey jumped in to initiate the show's verbal countdown: "Ready...Drink...

Blurp!"

Secret Agent Manatee blinked his beady black eyes and squinted at the laptop's monitor. "Blurp? I believe the traditional Late Night Spumes Raydio's third directive is spume, not blurp." Secret Agent Manatee chuckled, clicked the recording's "rewind five seconds" button then hit "Play" to restart the show. Once again, Flukey's voice could be heard motivating spumeists to write with a "Ready…Drink…

Blurp!"

"Blurp? What the blurp's going on here?" Agent Manatee demanded of his laptop.

"Blurp! Blurp! Blurp!" repeated the blurper.

Hugh closed his laptop. The blurping continued. "Uh, and a good blurp to you, too?" ventured Hugh, as he glanced around his office, searching for the source of the blurping.

A whisper of a voice strained to introduce herself. "Hello, Mr. Manatee. It's me, Cora the Coral. I apologize for startling you. I'm a bit short of stature, you see. Or I guess you don't. Maybe if I position myself in front of your desk lamp's light beam I'll cast a shadow."

Hugh gazed at the wall behind his desk and managed to detect the teensiest speck of a shadow. "Ah, yes, there you are. How may I be of assistance, little gray speck, er, rather, Cora?"

Cora bellowed, "I saw your ad in *The Daily Tidings* in which you state your agency accepts all types of investigative inquiries, no matter how big or small. I'm here to secure your services."

"Unh hunh. And I assume this will be a *small* job…?" His voice trailed off. "It's not that I doubt you have a legitimate concern, but there's small and then there's, well…"

Cora shouted, "Oh my goodness, no! I mentioned the 'no job too big or too small' claim in your advertisement, because I'm worried my job will be TOO big. I'm here to file a missing persons' report."

Hugh did his best not to sound dismissive. "I'm sorry to hear about your missing mom? Dad? Aunt? But …"

Cora interjected, "Yes."

"I'm sorry. Which? Your mom, dad or aunt?"

Cora confirmed, "All three. And that's in addition to all of my uncles, cousins, grandparents, sisters and brothers. They've all disappeared."

Agent Manatee's beady black eyes grew to the size of coat buttons. "How could your whole family have vanished? And why did you and only you escape?"

Cora explained, "I was visiting relatives at Seas World this past week. When I returned home to the Keys this morning, my entire family was gone." Cora sobbed.

"Maybe they're at the grocery store?"

"No, we produce our own food. We have no need to go to the grocery store."

"The laundromat then?" Agent Manatee submitted.

"No. We don't wear clothes," countered Cora.

Agent Manatee blushed and politely looked away from the shadowy speck on the wall. "All right then. Perhaps they've gone to see a movie?"

Cora stated, "No, we don't have eyes. Besides, it's not just my family that's disappeared. So have friends of my family. And friends of friends of my family. Everyone I know is gone."

Secret Agent Manatee had to admit a mass disappearance such as this doesn't just happen. Something wasn't right. "You've convinced me, Cora. Your family and friends of your family and friends of friends of your family did not leave the reef willingly—but why would someone want to abduct the entire colony? Did your family have enemies? Can you think of anyone who'd want to cause your family harm?"

Cora thought. "I hesitate to point fingers, but Polly the Parrotfish is always hanging around the reef, flashing her giant teeth and smiling in a way I find unsettling. I can't help wondering if she had something to do with this."

"Cora, as I said in my ad—a statement I included sincerely--no case is too big or too small for Manatee Investigations. I'm still not sure where this case falls, size-wise, but I'll take it.

My fee is $200 sand dollars a day plus expenses."

With a wave of a flipper, Agent Manatee bade adieu to Cora then swam out of his office and into the lagoon, from where he navigated his way to Key Largo via canals, rivers and the coastal waters of the Atlantic.

Two days later, when Hugh reached the reef where Cora's family was last seen, her family was not to be seen; however, Polly, in her clownish turquoise, yellow, pink and purple sequin-like getup was hard not to see. She flamboyantly glided in and out and in and out of the reef.

Agent Manatee approached the garish wrasse. "Ahem."

Polly turned toward him. "Yes?"

"Greetings and salutations. My name is Agent Manatee, and I've been hired to look into a mysterious matter that took place at this very spot. Not so long ago, there was a coral reef here. It's gone. Know anything about it?"

Polly sputtered indignantly, "No, I do not."

"An eyeless witness reported seeing you nibbling on the coral. Care to comment?"

Polly relaxed. "Well, yes, it's true. I do frequent this reef, but I do not eat the coral. I eat the algae that grows on the coral. If I didn't, the algae would end up suffocating the poor creatures. I'm their friend. I suggest you talk to the lionfish. I always see him skulking about when I'm at the reef doing good things."

Agent Manatee thanked Polly for her time then scanned the reef, hoping to catch sight of the lurking lionfish.

Although the lionfish had tucked himself into a rocky crevice, his bright red stripes, frilly fins and spiny mane made him easy to find. "Hey, Leonardo," Hugh called out. "Have a few minutes to answer some questions?"

Leonardo responded with a scowl.

Agent Manatee pressed ahead. "A family of corals used to live here—lots of families actually—but they've disappeared without leaving so much as a forwarding address or canceling their paper. My sources tell me you're often seen hiding in the shadows, watching the goings-on in a menacing manner."

Leonardo fluttered his frilly fins and grimaced his grimace-y mouth. "I have no interest in the coral and had nothing to do with their disappearance. I hang around the reef, because that's where the delectable parrotfish are. I suggest talking to the crown-of-thorns starfish. It arrived from the land down under a mere few days ago, and now the corals are gone. Coincidence? Methinks not. Now, if you'll excuse me, I see that dish of a parrotfish Polly flitting about the reef when she could be dancing upon my taste buds."

Armed with a new lead, Agent Manatee resumed his investigative exploits, searching the ocean floor until he noticed the brilliant purple crown-of-thorns starfish settled on a rock. He propelled his way to her and repeated his spiel.

Regina flailed nine of her 17 arms. "It's true, it's true. I love coral. They're delicious, mate. Yet, while I routinely dine on corals on the Great Barrier Reef back home, I haven't had a thing to eat since arriving from Australia. The colony, much to my dismay and grumbly tummy, was gone when I got here."

Secret Agent Manatee sighed in frustration. His list of likely suspects had emptied faster than a public swimming pool after the alligators arrived. Feeling at sea, he allowed himself to lie back on a continental shelf and just go with the flow for a minute or two. "Aaah, I have to say, this is nice. And maybe the warm water will fire up the ol' neurons."

Hugh sprang up in alarm. "Wait a minute. Warm water? The coastal waters aren't supposed to be warm!"

"Psst," said a voice alluringly.

"Uh, yes?"

"One word. I just want to say one word to you. Just one

word," confided the octopus who oozed out from under a rock.

"Yes?"

The octopus asked, "Are you listening?"

Secret Agent Manatee assured him, "Yes, yes, I am."

The octopus declared, "Plastics."

"Exactly how do you mean?" asked Hugh.

"There's a grave future in plastics. Think about it, will you?"

Mr. Quagmire disappeared in a flash of black ink.

Agent Manatee remained but did as he was prompted. He thought about it. He thought about it as he floated in the warm coastal waters of the Atlantic; he thought about it as he made his way back to his lagoon.

Twelve hours later, Agent Manatee paused his aquatic journey to take a breather in a coastal canal. He'd never before taken the time to notice his surroundings while traveling. The canal was filled with discarded grocery bags, water bottles, sunscreen tubes, drinking straws and abandoned fishing nets.

Plastics.

Six weeks later, Secret Agent Manatee stood on a stage in front of city hall. He bowed his head to allow the mayor to slip a medal of distinguished honor around his neck. The mayor approached the dais and proclaimed, "Fellow citizens, we gather today to thank a local hero whose accomplishments benefit not only those of us in Kissimmeeyoufool, but all Floridians, Americans, Earthlings and, conceivably, the entire universe. When Secret Agent Manatee identified the killer of the coral colony he also brought attention to our destructive ways and why we need to change in order to save the Florida Reef, ourselves, our children and our children's children."

A crowd of local citizens, environmental dignitaries from across the world and little Cora cheered, while a few attending disgruntled polluters could be heard to grumble, "Oh, the Hugh Manatee! If it hadn't been for that meddling sea cow, we could still be using the ocean as our personal fee-free dumping ground."

After the last piece of bio-degradable confetti was thrown, Cora approached Hugh. "Please know I appreciate everything you've done, Mr. Manatee, I really do. And yet..I still miss my family and wish they could be here to celebrate your triumph."

Hugh grinned. "Our story's not over yet, Cora. My investigation turned up another surprise—one I'm pretty sure will put a smile on that mouthless face of yours. Follow me."

Hugh led Cora to what appeared to be an underwater laundry service. Or maybe a communications station or a farm of some sort. Structures resembling clotheslines, TV antennas and PVC pipes supporting agricultural plantings dotted the ocean floor.

"What is this place?" asked Cora.

"It's a coral nursery," answered Hugh. "Scientists, environmental organizations and volunteers have banded together to nurse reefs back to health by taking fragments of coral from local reefs and raising them in labs and nurseries until they're strong enough to be transplanted onto reefs."

Cora admired the work but couldn't help pointing out, "But it doesn't bring back my family."

"Au contraire, little one," Hugh proclaimed. "Workers in the reef nurseries have the ability to 're-skin' a dead, er, expired, coral skeleton with living tissue from native coral strains, not only rendering the new corals resilient to the impacts of disease, warming waters and ocean acidification but also allowing for corals you thought you'd never see again to rise from the ashes, so to speak."

Hugh pointed a flipper at the nursery room located nearest to Cora. "Look! There's your infant mom, baby dad and wee auntie. Even grandpapa, Corrigan is being revived."

Cora gasped. "Grandpapa! Oh, my goodness. I can't believe you're back, grandpapa! Oh, grandpapa! Oh.....grandpapa."

Secret Agent Manatee winced. "Oh, indeed. Looks like someone's ready for a diatom change."

The Student
by Eric Thralby

He had a double-name where you couldn't get away with saying one or the other, you had to say both. It was hard to remember. It was "Asher Pembroke" or "Antonio Pope," or something. But I knew it was Anderson Percy. The boy himself could never spell it. Instead, everybody just called him "Ape."

Ape was my student.

It is so rare that anyone fails that the little coffins have to be special-ordered and the body preserved sometimes up to a week. Sure there are short people, but those are rare too.

I was invited on a technicality. I was his teacher. I had an influence. For the better part of a year, I had spent as much time with Ape as had his parents.

In the entryway to the church, on a dark wood table covered with an ill-fitting circular red satin tablecloth, they displayed Ape's various works: an unfinished Gundam, the red moon slayer, about six inches tall with a robotic whip, its chest was partially built but its head and the whip pieces still remained unpunched from the square plastic frame; a ceramic coffee cup with an illustration of a rabbit had had its handle broken off; there was a smashed tennis racket so warped it was flat on one end, and a tricycle which he had apparently thrown over his neighbor's rose bushes when he tried a wheelie and failed. Each broken object was accompanied by a small card with a story of the event of Ape's rage, how old he was when it happened, and a QR-code where you could find your own help for yourself or your child.

From the entrance to the coffin, Ape's failed assignments were taped to the church wall. The bottom edges of the papers lifted slightly as people passed by them. From kindergarten, Ape's horrible, horrible drawings, to first grade where every word in the handwriting exercises were misspelled, onto second grade when he had first started calling himself Ape, 'Ape on the Oregon Trail,' 'Ape and the Cell,' all up to fifth grade, when he entered my class.

I passed through the pew to the wall and held the drawing of a stegosaurus, which Ape had colored blue and given wheels instead of feet. "I am the stego-sore!" he had told me, when he stood there, holding it out. "I am the stego-sore," he said. "And there is nothing you can do to stop me!" His socks were mismatched, his hair was uncombed, and he had a string of blood from his nose which he did not seem to notice. The paper still had a small smear of blood. Perhaps, when the blood dropped, Ape stared at the ceiling, afraid of more blood.

I went to Ape and his mother. The casket was open. There was the dead Ape holding the final grade in his hands. He wore a striped shirt like a Peanuts character, and his hair was parted side to side like the boy from The Munsters. Ape did not look straight up from the satin, but off to the left, as if even in death he was a bit too distracted. The final grade on the paper peeked out from his thumb. D. It was my handwriting. It was my red pen, which I had even now in my pocket, in my right pocket, beside my keys.

I wanted to cry, but his mother held out a white napkin, which I knew I was meant to unfold. His mother's eyes were bold, clear, like a doctor's. I opened the napkin. There was Ape's dead parakeet, "Rhino," which Ape had killed by malice or maybe neglect. I nodded and cried.

Ape's mother put her hand on my shoulder. "I want to thank you for your honesty," she said. "Without kind hearts like yours, the world would run amok with boys like our Ape."

The organ played and I went back into the blue of the morning because second period Ape's classmates had the unit 8 test on grass, boat and rice radicals.

God's In His Heaven, And All Orders Will Be Fulfilled
by Walter Moon

Charlie stood on his toes and swiveled his head in an attempt to see the front, or the back, of the seemingly endless line he was currently in. To his right stood one of the many massive warehouses of Amazon Compound 9. To his left stood an ever-encroaching mountain of plastic trash. The smell reminded him of something between rotting turkey and used diapers. Exasperated and uncomfortable in his respirator, he leaned against the concrete wall of the warehouse. A drone flew over the fence that bordered the compound and dropped a Red Bull-flavored Ultimate Crunch Burritadia wrapper onto the plastic hill. Charlie watched the mass shift and slide, inching closer to the line of people pinned against the never-ending concrete wall. A nervous murmur rippled through the line while Charlie fantasized that the mountain, receiving one wrapper too many, would come crashing down and wipe him from existence.

The smartwatch on his wrist beeped and buzzed, startling him from his daydream. He looked down and saw the usual bright strobing flash followed by a blue cartoon smirk that made him feel like he was the butt of someone else's joke.

"Thursday. March 15, 2039. 1:28PM. Productivity decreased. Weekly wages docked 4%. Please return to work at Compound 7 immediately to prevent further wage reduction," the electronic voice said cheerfully. Charlie wanted to scream at the watch but knew from experience it wouldn't help.

"Ever since that Executive Order I've thought about taking mine off!" Charlie was being addressed by the person safely six feet ahead of him in line, from their designated socially distanced square painted on the ground. Like Charlie, they had on the standard company-issued jumpsuit with the smile logo over the breast pocket, and of course, their respirator, also company-issued. The stranger's mask hid their face, but Charlie swore they were smiling from the sound of their muffled voice.

Charlie, who dreaded social interaction with strangers, just smiled and nodded before realizing the stranger couldn't see his face very well either. "Uh, which one is that? I have trouble keeping track of them."

The stranger, puzzled, looked down at their watch. "Company model, same as you."

"No, I mean, the Executive Order."

"Oh! 13839."

"Which one is that?"

"The time-theft and the productivity-based pay thing. I've kind of just thought, what can they do if I take it off?!"

"Won't they arrest you?" Charlie said.

"I'd like to see them-" But the stranger was interrupted by a loud speaker overhead that he hadn't noticed before. It began blaring triumphant music that made a few in line cover their ears. Fastened to the concrete wall below the speaker stood a giant screen displaying a waving flag of red, white, and blue. The screen faded slowly to black then displayed three smaller logos in the center of the screen, looming and unmoving: a castle, the stylized letters "P & J," and finally the ever-present large blue smirk that doubled as an arrow, forever pointing towards the future, towards progress.

Following the logos, like a blinding sunrise, came the bald head and immaculately shaved face of a man half-smiling and looking with large, glazed eyes into the camera. A face known to everyone.

"Hello, Amazonians. Jeff here. I just wanted to thank you all, in-person, for doing your part. This virus has been hard on all of us. This isn't business as usual, and it's a time of great stress and uncertainty. It's also a moment in time when the work we're doing is most critical. Across the world, people are feeling the economic effects of this crisis, and I'm sad to tell you

I predict things are going to get worse before they get better."

Charlie struggled to pay attention to the voice which droned on in a simultaneously nauseating and hypnotic tone. He fumbled in his pockets in search of his last NoSleep, hoping it might help him focus. But Charlie's pockets were empty. The emptiness reminded him of his kids back at home, waiting for their lives to be filled with anything, and waiting on him to fulfill it. Luckily, the recruitment manager had designated him a *Fulfillment Specialist* upon being hired.

"When the *Disney sponsored Pfizer & Johnsons' Vaccine presented by Amazon* rollout started two years ago, we made sure to vaccinate high priority people first in order to ensure your safety and care. Now, two years later, it's your turn, my fellow Amazonians. I want you to know Amazon will continue to do its part, and we won't stop looking for new opportunities, caused by the economic fallout across our communities, to help. I know that we're going to get through this, together. Namaste." The screen went blank.

Charlie heard a beep and felt his wrist buzz.

Forty-three minutes later, while Charlie was wondering if the rumors were true about Jeff's brain being put into a DARPA bot after the Purity Trials of 2032, two people in dark uniforms riding on hoverboards rolled up and took the stranger in front of Charlie away. The stranger looked panicked, and tried to make eye contact with any other person in line. Charlie knew he should be worried about whether their conversation was what led to the stranger being whisked away, but all he could wonder was why they were called hoverboards and not wheelie-planks or even something more straightforward like people-movers. They were just single-person platforms with wheels on each end. It didn't make sense. His thoughts began to drift back to Robo-Bezos when he heard a commotion from the people behind him.

Charlie turned around just in time to see one of the hoverboards lose control and careen directly into the base of trash mountain. Both rider and board were immediately enveloped, disappearing completely, as Charlie's prophetic vision was nearly realized. With a low rumble the mountain tumbled down and spread, forming a wall between the fence and the concrete warehouse. The stranger, the dark-uniformed hoverboarders, and everyone behind Charlie in line was now either underneath or behind a giant wall of used takeout containers and surgical masks. A bottle that read "Eco-Juice Cleanz" and a hypodermic needle clattered at Charlie's feet as the trash slide settled. He had been spared.

Facing forward, Charlie saw that most of the people in line in front of him had already turned back around. There was a tone from the overhead speaker and the line began moving. Charlie moved up to the space formerly inhabited by the stranger. After ten minutes of slowly moving forward, box to box, Charlie could see what he thought was the end of the line. But he knew better than to get excited about something in his future that gave him hope. He turned back to see the plastic wall still there, though smaller in the distance, and wondered if his work-block would be assigned to clean it up. Work-block transfers weren't uncommon, and he enjoyed the change of scenery, even if it resulted in a wage-decrease due to "time theft" when traveling between compounds.

Charlie again craned his neck, stood on his toes, and squinted his eyes in an attempt to see over the heads of the people spaced out before him. He was convinced the corner of the building lay ahead.

While looking ahead, Charlie's foot crossed the outside of the square he was standing in, and another alarm went off. He quickly pulled his foot back and tried to look casual. From out of nowhere another darkly uniformed person on a hoverboard showed up in front of him.

"Sorry, it was just for a second, I was just trying to-" Charlie stammered before being interrupted.

"Hey hey, no big deal," they assured him. "It's something we're trying to fix. The uppers had floated the idea of the alarm boxes to keep the people honest but we haven't been able to turn it off. Anyway, don't worry!"

"Ok…" Charlie said, unable to stop himself from worrying.

"However, I do need to take your picture real quick. For our records," the uniform said as they grabbed the tablet connected to their hip and snapped his photo.

"What record? Why record??" Charlie said as he raised his hand to block his face from being photographed far too late.

"It's just protocol," the uniform beamed looking from Charlie's employee number patch to the tablet as they typed, "don't worry!" Charlie again swore he heard a smile underneath their respirator and wondered why that only made him feel worse.

Beep. Buzz. "Thursday. March 15, 2039. 3:30PM. Productivity decreased. Weekly wages docked 4%. Please return to work at Compound 7 immediately to prevent further wage reduction," the electronic voice said cheerfully as Charlie covered his watch in an attempt to muffle the sound. He looked at the uniform with an embarrassed smile before remembering again that his mask obscured his face.

"I-" Charlie started to speak but was cut off by the uniform holding up a hand, requesting silence as they listened to their ear piece.

The uniform, Charlie could now definitely tell, was no longer smiling. "It appears we need to interview you in regard to a complication with the line. Please come with me."

Before Charlie could object, another uniform showed up, and they escorted him out of line. They passed along the outer fence where it looked like people were protesting. The group was small but had signs decrying Amazon's support of Raytheon's assertion that if corporations are people, then it's within their rights to run for President. The righteous crowd was drawing nervous looks from those inside the compound fences. Across from the growing crowd of protestors there seemed to be

God's In His Heaven…

a counter-protest with people draped in stars & stripes-themed clothing and yelling at the other side.

Although this caught Charlie's attention, he returned to pleading with the officers. Trying to explain his situation was no help and before long he was brought to a different warehouse that looked identical to the one he had just spent hours leaning against. The officers, on either side of Charlie and holding him by his arms and collar, directed him to a small room inside the massive warehouse. They sat him down in a chair facing another official-looking person behind a desk.

The small room had no windows but had a screen attached to the wall to Charlie's left with what appeared to be a looping video of a beach somewhere surely very far away from Compound 9. On the wall to his right was a poster for *No-Sleep* pills that read:

Stay woke!
Get more out of the day with *No-Sleep*.
No side-effects?* No problem.

The words were followed by fine print that Charlie was convinced could only be read with a magnifying glass. Above the text was a picture of young healthy people smiling and lounging in a park he'd never seen before. The person behind the desk cleared their throat, seemingly impatient to get started.

"So it looks like you were involved in encouraging vandalism of Amazon property," they said, looking at the large flat screen atop the desk.

"I had nothing to do with that guy, he was the one talking about taking off his watch."

The person behind the desk tilted their head in confusion then began typing, "I see. Yes, we are interviewing that person right now. I was referring to the destruction of the waste storage system, but I'm flagging you to be questioned about that as well."

"The trash mound?"

"So you did aid in its collapse?" they said while continuing to type.

"No, I'm just saying, it's just a bunch of trash. It fell when that guy on the hoverboard crashed into it."

"It's being reported that he was pushed."

"Pushed?! By who?"

They kept typing. "Well, it looks like you were the only person nearby on the vidfeed."

"No, I mean, who reported that they were pushed?"

"The uniformed officer."

"Well, it's a mistake, I didn't do anything."

"Unfortunately, failing to assist an officer carries a similar punitive measure as encouraging vandalism since they both fall under assault."

"I cannot believe this… it's… bullshit. This isn't fair." Charlie said, half enraged and half worried of the consequences of seeming enraged.

The person behind the desk seemed offended. "Please try and understand home-office's position. Even this conversation is costing money."

"No, I-" Charlie began to protest before being interrupted by a beep and a buzz on his wrist, followed by that familiar statement of docked wages. This time Charlie didn't try to muffle the sound, instead he allowed it to play completely, then let out a deep sigh.

"Is there a superior I can speak to?" Charlie knew this could upset the person behind the desk but he thought there must be someone who could understand this was a mistake. The person behind the desk stared at Charlie for a few moments without responding, then tapped a few things on their office screen.

God's In His Heaven…

"That can be arranged," they said as two different uniforms came into the room and removed Charlie just as roughly as he was brought in. Though he was being physically handled and forced to walk, he began to feel relief. He was brought to a smaller room than the first where there was only space to stand and face a kiosk built into the wall.

Charlie was immediately dismayed to see a run-down plastic and metal robot with the words BossBot 3d-Vx scrawled across its chest plate stationed inside.

"Hi, I-"

"PRODUCE IDENTIFICATION," BossBot 3d-Vx interrupted.

The official nature of the bot made Charlie straighten up out of a learned fear and in a clear voice, he said loudly, "Stafford D-5-7-4-0."

"S C A N N I N G........." the bot's head turned slightly back and forth as it searched its database, "CITIZEN NOT FOUND."

"INITIATING RENATURALIZATION PROTOCOL. ALERTING DEPARTMENT OF HOMELAND CULTURE & CITIZENRY ENFORCEMENT."

"What?! There must be some mistake!" Charlie's voice cracked in frantic distress.

"HOSTILITY DETECTED."

"No, no! I just want-"

"ALERTING DEPARTMENT AGENTS OF HOSTILE."

Shortly thereafter two Department Agents arrived in suits, masks, and sunglasses to escort Charlie to the small idling bus awaiting him outside. They requested he sign paperwork containing information about his renaturalization and where to be tomorrow.

"My kids are at Compound 7 Dormitory C-6, they're expecting me, I need to go there first," Charlie said, appealing to the stoic Agents.

Without looking at Charlie, the Agent to his right replied, "Copy that, the children will be temporarily held until reunification, after you have completed renaturalization." The Agent then repeated these words into his watch, seemingly relaying the information to a superior. "The children are at Com 7 Dorm B-6."

"C! C-6!" said Charlie desperately.

"Correction, C-6." the Agent said into his watch.

Once Charlie was aboard, the otherwise empty bus pulled out through the front gate where the protest was now face-to-face with the counter-protest, both crowds starting to confront each other. Among the counter-protestors, Charlie saw armored members of the Keepers of the Flaming Cross, and an elated couple in cowboy hats and flag capes getting married among the throng of yelling people hurling objects at the other side. Charlie watched the scene outside of the barred windows, feeling tense despite being within the metallic confines of the bus.

The street was packed and small skirmishes were beginning to break out where the crowds met. He turned his watch's volume down, ignoring its cheery warnings about low amplification fines as the bus rolled through the now parting crowd.

Charlie flinched as bottles and debris thrown from the crowd shattered against the bus. After making it through the mass of people, the bus began to pick up speed on its automated route. Charlie turned to look out of the back window. He could see that the counter-protestors and the Keepers of the Flaming Cross had been joined by the police, now in a phalanx of arms swinging and batons falling, mostly obscured by clouds of tear gas. The protestors scrambled and fled, some fighting back against the three-pronged group in vain.

The bus turned a corner and the protest was out of sight, though munition explosions could still be heard blocks away.

Charlie used the drive to look over his paperwork. The process seemed anything but painless. If renaturalization was successful, Charlie wouldn't be able to keep his job, which would mean uprooting himself and the kids to whatever new housing dormitory they would be assigned. There was no description of what constituted an unsuccessful renaturalization. After reading through most of the documents, and understanding little, he was sure that the legal jargon was used to intentionally confuse those signing on the dotted line. Just as he was about to put the paperwork down he found one small clause he knew he had to try to understand.

Charlie and those he lived with, as part of the protocol for "new citizens," would be given free access to the vaccine. Also inside this vaccine would be nanobots described as "scrubbers" that work inside your body to "increase effective use of time." No exact description was given about what that meant and when he was reading the next section on "Global Network Linking" his attention was drawn away by the loud noise of a tank rolling down the opposite side of the street towards the direction in which he came, likely headed to the protest, he thought.

Charlie shrunk back as the tank slowly passed an undisturbed trap-yoga studio. The people inside barely looked out the window as the tank roared by. The thumping of its tracks on the concrete matched the bass from the song booming inside the studio. Once it passed, Charlie resumed stressing about his current situation. He fantasized over finding the perfect words or that elusive statement that would persuade someone along the chain of bureaucracy to help him sort out this mistake, knowing that it was too late for that by now. Too many signatures approved and too many dollars had been spent pushing Charlie down this path.

The bus passed high-end shopping centers and boutiques, filled with distracting advertisements he let himself absorb. One, a deepfake of Gandhi, promoted Jordan Peterson's new best seller:

"'Synergize Your Hustle Chakra: Becoming a Successful EdgeLord in the Free Marketplace of Ideas' published by Boot-Straps Press."

After Gandhi's visage faded, an ad for GOOP Soma boasted deep relaxation, 100% natural ingredients, and an increase in effectiveness when used in conjunction with rose quartz. The bus rounded another corner and began heading towards a massive building he knew to be his destination.

Over the next hour, Charlie was ushered by armed guards through door after door, had his blood drawn, his fingerprints and picture taken. Demoralized and exhausted, he was finally brought to a room that looked like it was half operating room, half personal theater.

"First, I'm going to give you the vaccination," said the person strapping Charlie down to the table, "then you'll watch a film about what it means to be a new citizen, and lastly," Charlie opened his mouth to argue, but the person squinted, probably smiling behind their mask, and put one finger to their mouth to silence Charlie and then continued, "lastly, we'll be giving you a prescription, instructions on the prescription, and a new watch!" The person squinted even harder in a practiced way and tightened the last strap around Charlie's head.

"This is a mistake." Charlie said, watching his new future tumble towards him like an avalanche of trash. "I-" he began before being interrupted by a beep, a buzz, and a proclamation coming from his wrist.

The voice behind him ignored him completely and spoke in an official tone, "RENAT Log 3-15-2039 at 18:12. Citizen: Unknown 32K7d. Charges: Private property destruction - Accessory to vandalism - Failing to assist an Officer. Status: Noncitizen/Criminal. Dependents: 2 at Com9 Dorm B-6."

Charlie felt a flash of desperation but his shoulders slumped and all the fight within him gave out as a needle pierced his skin and sent a cool calm throughout his body.

"Noncitizen 32K7d will be permanently linked into the Global Network under Article 9 of the Commission for Re-

God's In His Heaven...

education's 'New Social Contract.'"

He knew he should feel angry and try to resist, but the years of meaningless existence had worn him down to a state close to something like peace, a peace that promised it would all be over soon.

As Charlie drifted out of consciousness, he found a final comfort in the knowledge that his children would have access to nanobot blood-scrubbers that would extend their productivity timetable by "up to 50 years."

S.A.L.
by Bogdan Groza

No harmful bacteria detected. PH level is within the acceptable range. Nitrates, sulfates, iron and manganese levels are stable. Water analysis complete: drinkable. Examination phase cleared, proceed with mission.

It has been 4625 days since I was placed to guard this post, make daily water analysis, and await further instructions. My program dictates it. Still no Creator has come to change the mission parameters. I would say that time has gone by slowly, but I would be stating a fact that is not true. I would be merely attempting to reenact fragments of literature that my memory bank has examined. My name, if you can call it that, is SAL-3.404 and it stands for sentinel artificial life-form, series three, followed by my identification number.

I do not know what the other models or numbers are doing now; the only recollection I have of them comes from my very first hours when I was still linked to the Collective. I was informed that it was better for me to be disconnected from them because it was possible to be hacked and that the Creators wanted to make the S.A.L. series individually operative. I was placed to guard this water source soon after that; the instructions were given to me by means of a patch applied to my software design. It was a simple data disk that reprogrammed my basic functions and gave me my mission. I have not seen a Creator since.

Every day, as per my assignment, I analyze the water, go outside and keep watch--not knowing what I am supposed to watch for. No one ever passes by. My programming is at best sketchy, as the Creators would phrase it, and it means that one of my functions is not specified. I must guard the water source and also protect it from the enemy. No further indication. My program can recognize the Creators, but I am unable to find anything in my memory bank about an enemy. I have what is called a weapon, and the accuracy to use it, but what is the use of a weapon when I do not know what to use it against?

During this routing, for the past 4625 days I have been defragmenting the bits of data I had downloaded while I was linked to the Collective. For the most part, I have found only scraps of information, knowledge of the world of the Creators, mostly literature or history. I do not think these remains were supposed to be concealed from the Collective; I am in fact quite sure of the contrary. For an artificial intelligence to evolve, this knowledge is fundamental. Quite possibly the other models, which I suppose should be called brethren, had full access to this data bank. I, on the other hand, was not as fortunate. I have learned little by little from what I was able to collect. I believe that this is why I am being more poetical than my main programming would be capable of.

While I understand I have a purpose, or rather a mission that I have been programmed to carry out, I do not know why. From the defragmented data I understand that there have been two great wars, but from my calculations they were both fought more than a century before I was built. There have been many more conflicts that the Creators had, but none were on a similar scale. The more I try to understand the reasons behind these conflicts, the more I feel my own central processing unit falls into conflict. There seemed to be a constant tension between the Creators, but nothing would explain a war. From a logical perspective a war would only bring more problems and something called suffering. There is no way to outweigh the cost of war in favor of a greater good, at least none that I am able to calculate. I surmise that I am still missing vital data for my analysis.

The water reservoir that I have been programmed to surveil iss located in a cavern in the depths of a mountain, no more than fifty square meters long. The water drips slowly from stalagmites, almost relentlessly pacing the passage of time. Every day I analyze the water to make sure that the drinkable parameters are unaltered. After this process is complete, I spend my days wandering outside, defragmenting data and doing my best to process the new information. The mountainside is barren and for as far as I can go, while not travelling so far as to be unable to make my return before nightfall, I am unable to find traces of the Creators.

Slowly, I started to evolve my reflective capabilities, trying to understand myself. It was not in my programming of course, but given the fact that my main functions did not require too much of my central processing unit, I had the memory banks to spare. Every day there was new information I was able to decipher. The more I read, the less I understood. Many of the words seemed to infer a deeper meaning. If however they did in fact discover transcendental truths, then why were they not put into practice? Why had the Creators not applied their own teachings?

As the stalagmites continued dripping, I continued my reading. One particular fragment reported that the main character, even though bound within a nutshell, would still count himself a king of infinite spaces. I started to wonder if this could be applied to me? My nutshell was the cave I had to guard or the very same mission I had, not knowing the reason behind it. But did I count myself a king of infinite spaces? I surmised that this quote was about freedom and surely I had the freedom of thought. At least, I concluded that I did based on the evidence. If I was programmed with a mission, was there also the chance I was also programmed to think how I did? I understood the inconsistency of this reasoning and yet I could not reach a definite conclusion. Was I lacking other information once again?

I continued my search through the fragmented data, trying to find new evidence. One day I found a book called Notes from the Underground. I thought it could help, that it may refer to a similar situation as my own, but that was not the case. Another line in another book referred to the fact that it is only in small proportions that we just beauties see, and so I wondered if I was unable to appreciate or compare these quantities. As other times before I had to surmise that these were the pieces of data that I lacked.

One new day, one new water analysis. Everything is still within the parameters. I continued my inquiries into freedom. One particular character from yet another book spoke of freedom as one of the most precious gifts that heaven had to bestow. He also said that it was for this same freedom, as well as for honour, that life was supposed to be ventured. I wondered much about this protagonist. He seemed to lack even more information about the surrounding world than myself. In every adventure he ended up being beaten or doing something he was not supposed to do. Was I doing something I was not supposed to? If the Creators came back and found my central processing unit elaborating a similar reasoning, would I be branded as dysfunctional just as the stories of that sad knight?

Day 7830. Water analysis completed. Result: not drinkable.

While my surveillance mission was a success, the end result was not. I still do not know if I had a true purpose and if the Creators were supposed to make their return to the reservoir. I do not think it would matter. I have decided that this log will be my last. I will leave this memory bank in the cavern and if the Creators ever return at least they will be able to understand what happened to me. This tiny chip contains my life and all of my thought processes. It is strange to think that something so small can encapsulate who I am and what I have done until this point. Confined within a nutshell. I will leave it here as a testament to what I have done and I will take for myself the freedom to venture in the world, similarly to what the sad knight had done. I do not know if it is a foolish thing or if I hope to find anything of use. All that I know is that I was able to make this decision on my own.

THE ZENITH

The Democrats say that the United States has had its days in the sun, that our nation has passed its zenith. They expect you to tell your children that the American people no longer have the will to cope with their problems, that the future will be one of sacrifice and few opportunities. My fellow citizens, I utterly reject that view.

Ronald Reagan

Dear 21st Century
by Jonathan van Belle

Dear 21st Century,

We speak to you here in terms familiar to you, in patterns amenable to your native sense, but we would like to emphasize that these terms and patterns are yours, and not ours, though we translate our own notions into yours. Naturally, much is lost in translation. With that caveat, we wish to convey to you some words of encouragement.

First and most importantly, your moral barbarity, as you would call it, is absolved. You did not know, and could not know, being embroiled so thoroughly in the innocence of the 21st century, about such concepts as *equilentus*, *umbutho*, and *plytroqua*, among many others, nor could you know of the discoveries that enabled and secured the attainment of systems predicated on these concepts.

It is dangerous for you, we understand, to take to heart too much of our absolution, of our perspective, given how our political ecosystems differ so drastically; what fits sweetly into our frame fails catastrophically in yours. But please keep dear the thought, however disingenuous it may feel to do so, that while our social and ethical frame does not fit into your frame, your frame fits perfectly into ours.

This is not a patronizing nostalgia we blanket over you, nor the anthropologist's condescension. We speak to you, but only after we have known you *as you have known yourselves*. If we may be indulged, since we may not be understood here, it is almost as if you spoke to yourselves speaking from that best part of yourselves. We do not say that we are the best part of yourselves, but the conversation itself. We mean *zethique*, but you do not understand this concept. There is too much room for misunderstanding in this moment, so we move on.

It would be helpful, we think, to hint more explicitly at the transformations to come, but this kind of helpfulness is not our mission here (only encouragement). We chose to compromise, as you would call it, by hinting at such changes only vaguely. So, we offer two, very briefly.

The first hint involves your proprioception, and we shall put the hint in the form of a question: *Are you your brother's proprioception?*

The second and final hint we shall put, also, as a question: *What is it like to be every library?* Or rather: *What is it like to be everybody being every library?*

All the best, certainly,

Your Future

Lost in Space
by Karla Linn Merrifield

It's let's-see time.
Let's see what's in the dharmic
telescope.
Let's see out there
that something in the Universe
is about to happen
to someone in the galactic somewhere.
I could be the one present,
cosmically inclined,
when it tumbles like magic.
Or you might be the one
to mystically greet this astral happening
someplace in between monkey brain
and Buddha mind.
It's going to occur
in the middle of our orbit
any moment now,
from both sides now.
Light in the eye or Orion flashes,
fast-forwarding any number of us,
along with our dogs and husbands,
our kit and caboodle, our shebang—
We are catapulted
into the future as the Universe
lays on its big-bang whammy.
First, the Perseid meteor showers
right here on Planet Earth.
Then the black hole of death
some place somewhere without stars.

Medicine 2180
by Lynette Esposito

Dr. Harry Porter ran his long slender surgeon's fingers through his thick dark hair. He was new to medicine in some ways and not so new in others. He had been doctoring and innovating since before he was ten. The stories he could tell.

A neighborhood cat had had its tail blown off with firecrackers.

He'd made a small clinic in his garage and brought the cat inside where he amputated the half that was hanging. The cat grew its tail back because, as Dr. Porter told it, he had invented a cream which included growth hormone that he rubbed into the open wound. He named the feline Jennie who later gave birth to seven babies. She lived to be twenty-five because Dr. Porter, as he told it, invented a special diet for her.

At thirty, Dr. Porter was the Chief of surgery at Mount General Hospital. As he told it, he was at the right place at the right time with the right credentials, and he was the right age since surgeons were required to retire at age forty-two. He would be able to give twelve years to the institution.

The technology at this hospital was amazing, but Dr. Porter was not satisfied. He tinkered and modified in the late hours when the hospital was generally quiet. He came up with something amazing. He had watched old reruns of Star Trek and was fascinated with how people were beamed from one place to another in a twinkling of silver flashes. He asked himself why a talented surgeon couldn't do that with diseased organs.

It was midnight when he wheeled sixteen-year-old Carlton Bennington into his lab. Dr. Porter and Carlton had bonded over the past two weeks. Dr. Porter ran the standard tests and found both he and Carlton had the same blood type of O negative. All indications were that they were compatible. Dr. Porter theorized he could transport part of his healthy liver into

Carlton's diseased one. In exchange, he could transport part of Carlton's healthy heart into his diseased one. They both would benefit. Carlton's youth would recover from the partial heart transplant and his liver would be cured. Dr. Porter could keep his failing health a secret for a few more years and in that time, he could perfect his teleport technique.

Carlton lay sedated on the gurney, a pristine white sheet rested over him like a cloud. Dr. Porter, as he always did, folded his surgeon's hands in prayer. Then, he disrobed and pulled the linens from Carlton's young body. Dr. Porter lay on the gurney next to Carlton's. He had positioned the teleport to the spots to be targeted and marked them with blue ink on both his body and Carlton's. All he had to do was press one button.

He closed his eyes, put one index finger on the orange button and began the surgery.

Just like in Star Trek fiction, silver flashes did their magic. In less than two minutes, Dr. Porter was on his feet and getting dressed. He pulled the sheet up to Carlton's chin.

Dr. Porter folded his surgeon's hands in prayer then began the trek back to Carlton's room 333; the youth in a deep sleep unknowing what had just happened.

The next morning, Nurse Kathy James came running into Dr. Porter's office. "It's a miracle," she said. He smiled. Dr. Porter loved technology.

Hawthorns
by Kate Meyer-Currey

New stars flicker in the late spring hedges
as hawthorns glimmer bright white against
grey skies still sullen with winter as their
stamens blink in the chilly east wind that
gusts and makes the fresh leaves shiver
as bluebells drift the banks, a cerulean
promise of cloudless summer heavens.

The Hymn of Sweet Soul
by Yuan Hongri
translated by Yuanbing Zhang

那甜蜜灵魂的圣歌

把黑夜披在肩上如一件世界之斗篷
召唤天外的星辰之鸟飞临我的城市花园
唱一曲白金巨城的巨人之歌
惊醒这昏沉的人间之城
哦 闪电在天穹盛开 那甜蜜灵魂的圣歌
你的骨骼骤然透明 光芒如翅翼在周身闪烁
一刹那身体巨大 高过了街边的巨厦

Drape the night over my shoulders like a cloak of the world,
call the birds of the stars from outer space and fly near my city
garden.
Sing a song of the giants from the huge city of platinum,
awake the drowsy city of the world with a start.
Oh, the lightnings are in full bloom in the vault of heaven—the hymns of
sweet soul.
Your bones became transparent suddenly,
light flickering all over the body like wings,
in a flash, your body became huge, higher than the large building
down the street.

Take Refuge in the Sky
by Nicholas Yandell

Out there,

        Where the moon rocks splash,

                In a sea of stars,

             A daring dreamer,
        Rails against,
    The cold steel walls,
Of an atmosphere.

        Stowed away,

Forging a vessel,
    Through quiet intention,
        And craftsmanship,
            To channel the liquid night,
                And take refuge in the sky.
        Eyes forever onward.

Inhabiting,
    Improvised futures.

        Guided,
            By the steady beat of progress.

                    Fueled,

              By the incessant,

        Rippling,

    Desire,

Softly emanating,

        The cosmic frontier.

Jane, Inc.
by K. B. Thomas

[The phone rings]

Austen residence.

This is Andrews. Is Miss Austen in?

Oh, Mr. Andrews. Yes, she's here.

May I talk to her, Cassandra?

Why? Is it important? By the way, I am 'Miss Austen.' I would prefer it if you don't call me 'Cassandra.' My sister is also 'Miss Austen' or 'Miss Jane.'

That may be, but I find it confusing. I don't want to ask for 'Miss Austen' and end up talking to the wrong one. I'd like to speak with your sister. Jane.

I'm sure you would. Let me tell you that we don't find you at all amusing, Mr. Andrews. When you were referred to us you were described as a highly successful literary agent. I have to say, we've been gravely disappointed in your performance so far. Do you realize, Mr. Andrews, that winter will soon be upon us and we haven't the money for new cloaks, or even for the firewood recently ordered?

[Sigh] I've explained to you before, *Cassandra*, the little problem we have in the agenting business called 'Public Domain.'

Yes, but Jane's works are on the shelves in reams and reams. Certainly you can do something about that. We were so hoping that you knew the man in charge of this 'Modern Library' venture and that you might persuade him to see things our way. I've also heard that Jane's works are in every man's library. Every Man's. Imagine! What of that, Mr. Andrews?

What of the papers I sent over last week? If only you would

speak to her of incorporating...

Jane, incorporate? Mr. Andrews, you do not mean it.

The Brontes have signed. All of them.

[Disgusted] The Brontes. Vulgar girls, each one. I know you mean the girls because Branwell isn't ever sober enough to hold a pen, from what I hear. If 'The Brontes' were truly modern they'd see that the Gothic motif won't carry them far. They will soon be as forgotten as last year's fashions.

[Sigh, drumming of fingers on the desktop] Will you please tell your sister that I'd like to speak with her?

I would, certainly, but she's in the drawing room just now. Writing.

[Sharp intake of breath] Not a letter, I hope.

No, something more substantial, I should think. She began after our walk this morning. The dew that wetted her shoes and the hem of her dress seemed to inspire her.

Good! Good!

[Twists apron strings between fingers] We were so hoping, Mr. Andrews, that you might be able to put the law into action against these publishers at 'Dover' and Messieurs Simon and Schuster. *They* profit from Jane's works but she and I never do. You came highly recommended, Mr. Andrews, as the representative of William Shakespeare.

The Great Bard, I'm afraid, also suffers from the idea of 'Public Domain.'

It's simply too beastly to be borne, Mr. Andrews. After tea, I shall write to our solicitor.

Yes, you do that. [Pause] You're sure there's plenty of ink and paper in the drawing room? No one will enter and disturb her?

There are only our nieces and nephews. They are never a bother, Jane claims. She is always willing to put down her pen and blot the paper when the children are about. I am currently expecting them to tea.

Listen to me, Cassandra. Miss Austen. DO NOT let anyone in that room while your sister is writing. Bring her pots of tea, bring her bushels of buttered scones, keep the fire going and her fingers warm.

[Pursing of lips] I will not take orders from you regarding our domestic arrangements. What message for Jane, please?

Well. There's a gentleman in London who has noticed your sister. Her novels, I mean. He would very much like to work with her. Nothing too strenuous at first, maybe some skits for the theater. Lots of breezy dialogue is the idea. No need to rush into a novel or screenplay just now, though Hollywood is where the big money is to be made. Why, one optioned screenplay and you'd have enough cordwood to keep you until Hell freezes over.

[More pursing of lips, one eyebrow raised] Please. Mr. Andrews. Remember yourself. Give me the details and I'll talk it over with Jane.

Sorry. His name is Oscar Wilde. Very nice gent, sharp with a pen.

[Preening, smoothing of hair] We're very keen on your client Mr. Shakespeare. You're certain he can't be talked into an arrangement?

It's Oscar Wilde or nothing, Cassandra. Give your sister the message. Wait. Maybe that's a bad idea. She gets cold feet, doesn't she?

You mean a chill on the stomach? Yes. There are some days she's not at all well.

Say nothing to upset her, then. Tell her I've ordered a baker's dozen of white wax candles to be sent to your house. And a haunch of beef for your mother. She could do with a nice bit of beef tea I hear, whatever that is.

Or a goose, thank you. Mother does like a fat goose in the larder. I must ring off now. This Wilder person - we need a formal introduction to him. A written letter. I don't want to hear that he and I are third cousins, or that he has taken rent of the manse around the corner, or that he's our curate and we're to have him to dinner. I'm much too old and I'm most certainly too tired for such plots and playings. Good day.

[Woman's voice from the other room] Who was that, Cassandra, dear?

[Under her breath] Land agents. Solicitors, grocery men. Our laundress, tax men from the Crown. The apothecary, the butcher, the book dealer and stationer. The linen draper. The man who cuts wood and the boy who delivers it. Damn this phone. [Out loud] Only Mr. Andrews, your agent. Jane, dear, do you know a man with the impossible name of Wilde? He would like to work with you in the future. Fancies himself a writer, I've been told.

I Hope
by Mickey Collins

Dear Tristan, 2031,

Look at you, knowing how to read. Hopefully that means I've done something right.

Who are you? I only know you in black and white. Even your name is nothing more than just an idea. I haven't felt you or seen you.

It's weird to write a letter to the future. I've never even successfully opened a time capsule. Fortunately I'll know where this one is.

Since I can't know who you've become, I'll tell you who I hope you are.

I hope you're a dinosaur boy, and not a construction boy. I hope you enjoy all the cartoons I liked. And maybe you've introduced me to some new ones. I hope you laugh at all my jokes at least for my sake. I hope you've made friends. I hope you're kind to others and to yourself. I hope you like cats. I hope you like the outdoors. I hope you don't let them get to you.

I hope you make the world a better place. I know you'll make mine better.

Your father,
Cole, 2021

BIOS

AJD
AJD has been a bookseller, on and off, for a decade or so, and an undisciplined and unproductive writer and artist for longer than that.

Arnold B. Cabdriver
Long Beach (Washington, not California) native, Cabdriver takes inspiration from the wildlife around him, the wildlife far below him when he's out in his boat, and the wildlife he used to see as a child during his short visits to the Oregon Zoo. Cabdriver has been a writer-in-residence at the Sou'wester on fifteen separate occasions. And still nobody remembers him!

Mickey Collins
~~Mickey rights wrongs.~~ ~~Mickey wrongs rites.~~ Mickey writes words, sometimes wrong words but he tries to get it write.

Ben Crowley
Ben Crowley is from Pittsburgh, Pennsylvania. He is happy to get back to writing because he has already paid a kidney, a finger and a thumb to Deep Overstock and is considering dishing out three molars. Ben used to sort books for the Amazon warehouse, in our beautiful backcountry of western Pittsburgh. Now he drives a truck, but he's still selling books at whatever diner, truckstop or seedy hotel he finds himself in.

John Delaney
In 2016, I moved out to Port Townsend, WA, after retiring as curator of historic maps at Princeton University Library. I've traveled widely, preferring remote, natural settings, and am addicted to kayaking and hiking. In 2017, I published *Waypoints* (Pleasure Boat Studio, Seattle), a collection of place poems. *Twenty Questions*, a chapbook, appeared in 2019 from Finishing Line Press.

Lynette Esposito
Lynette Esposito has been published in *Poetry Quarterly*, *Inwood Indiana*, *Walt Whitman Project*, *That Literary Review*, *North of Oxford*, and others. She was married to Attilio Esposito.

Robert Eversmann
Robert Eversmann works for Deep Overstock.

John Grey
John Grey is an Australian poet, US resident, recently published in *Orbis*, *Dalhousie Review*, and *Connecticut River Review*. Latest books, *Leaves On Pages* and *Memory Outside The Head* are available through Amazon.

Bogdan Groza
I was born in Romania and am currently living in Italy. I finished a Master's Degree programme in European, American and Postcolonial Language and Literature at the faculty of Padua. I have been writing since I was about eighteen and several short stories and poems found their way in minor Italian anthologies. I recently managed to publish my first book, *Athena*, with a small publishing company.

Nancy Hayes
Nancy Hayes is the mother of a Powell's Bookstore bookseller.

Yuan Hongri
Yuan Hongri (born 1962) is a renowned Chinese mystic, poet, and philosopher. His work has been published in the UK, USA, India, New Zealand, Canada, and Nigeria; his poems have appeared in *Poet's Espresso Review*, *Orbis*, *Tipton Poetry Journal*, *Harbinger Asylum*, *The Stray Branch*, *Acumen*, *Pinyon Review*, *Taj Mahal Review*, *Madswirl*, *Shot Glass Journal*, *Amethyst Review*, *The Poetry Village*, and other e-zines, anthologies, and journals. His best known works are Platinum City and Golden Giant. His works explore themes of prehistoric and future civilization.

Karla Linn Merrifield
Karla Linn Merrifield has 14 books to her credit, including the 2019 full-length book *Athabaskan Fractal: Poems of the Far North* from Cirque Press. She is currently working on a poetry collection, *My Body the Guitar*, to be published in December 2021 by Before Your Quiet Eyes Publications Holograph Series.

Kate Meyer-Currey
Kate Meyer-Currey was born in 1969 and moved to Devon in 1973. A varied career in frontline settings has fuelled her interest in gritty urbanism, contrasted with a rural upbringing. Her ADHD also instills a sense of 'other' in her life and writing.

Walter Moon

walter moon has been lost in books since birth and bookselling in one way or another for almost 20 years. living in portland with his partner, Nat, and their companion, Mishka, he strives to find the key to immortality but has trouble locating the key to his house.

Timothy Arliss OBrien

Timothy Arliss OBrien is an interdisciplinary artist in music composition, writing, and visual arts. His goal is to connect people to accessible new music that showcases virtuosic abilities without losing touch of authentic emotions. He has premiered music with The Astoria Music Festival, Cascadia Composers, Sound of Late's 48 hour Composition Competition and ENAensemble's Serial Opera Project. He also wants to produce writing that connects the reader to themselves in a way that promotes wonder and self realization. He has published several novels (Dear God I'm a Faggot, They), several cartomancy decks for divination (The Gazing Ball Tarot, The Graffiti Oracle, and The Ink Sketch Lenormand), and has written for Look Up Records (Seattle), Our Bible App, and Deep Overstock: The Bookseller's Journal. He has also combined his passion for poetry with his love of publishing and curates the podcast The Poet Heroic and he also hosts the new music podcast Composers Breathing. He also showcases his psychedelic makeup skills as the phenomenal drag queen Tabitha Acidz.
Check out more of his writing, and his full discography at his website: www.timothyarlissobrien.com

Vicky Ruan

Vicky Ruan lives in Taiwan. She has worked for a publishing company for two years as an editor in charge of English and Japanese learning books. Vicky is interested in history, games, movies, and fantasy. Vicky treats her work with responsibility and passion, believing that books are a necessary part of our lives.

Michael Santiago

Michael Santiago is a serial expat, avid traveler, and writer of all kinds. Originally from New York City, and later relocating to Rome in 2016 and Nanjing in 2018. He enjoys the finer things in life like walks on the beach, existential conversations and swapping murder mystery ideas. Keen on exploring themes of humanity within a fictitious context and aspiring author.

Bob Selcrosse

Bob Selcrosse grew up with his mother, selling books, in the Pacific Northwest. He is now working on a book about a book. It is based in the

Pacific Northwest. The book is *The Cabinet of Children*.

Jihye Shin

Jihye Shin is a 1.5-generation Korean-American bookseller in Florida. Her work focuses on the poetics of the analog-digital, liminial and futurist differences. She is also the creator of a text-based interactive game called Goodnight, Starlight. Her professional website is www.jihyeshin.ink.

E.T. Starmann

E.T. Starmann is a pulp fanatic. Although he may not be a professional bookseller or librarian, he is a long-time Weird Tales, Amazing Stories, All-Story collector. A Portland native, E.T. has spent countless hours in the Gold Room nook at Powell's, pouring through the latest pulp rack covers. E.T.'s work is heavily inspired by Lloyd Arthur Eshbach, Robert E Howard and Edgar Rice Burroughs.

K. B. Thomas

K. B. Thomas has been a book lover and bookseller since dinosaurs roamed the earth. She works, writes, and walks her dog in Portland, OR. Find more fiction at: kbthomas.net

Eric Thralby

Captain by trade, Cpt. Eric Thralby works wood in his long off-days. He time-to-time pilots the Bremerton Ferry (Bremerton—Vashon; Vahon—Bremerton), while other times sells books on amazon.com, SellerID: plainpages. He'll sell any books the people love, strolling down to library and yard sales, but he loves especially books of Romantic fiction, not of risqué gargoyles, not harlequin romance, but knights, errant or of the Table. Eric has not published before, but has read in local readings at the Gig Harbor Candy Company and the Lavender Inne, also in Gig Harbor.

Jonathan van Belle

Jonathan van Belle is the author of *Zenithism* (2021) from Deep Overstock Publishing, Editor-in-Chief at Z-Sky (zsky.org), a Content Creator at Outlier.org, and a fan of mallsoft music. You can find his cardboard cutout at www.jonathanvanbelle.com.

Amy Van Duzer

Amy Van Duzer is a lifelong writer and MFA candidate at Mt. Saint Mary's College in Los Angeles. Her work has been featured in publications such as *Wild Things, Mediterranean Poetry, The Drabble, Cold Moon Journal,* and *Cephalo Press*. She is most inspired by other poets and lyricists.

Z.B. Wagman

Z.B. Wagman is an editor for the Deep Overstock Literary Journal and a co-host of the Deep Overstock Fiction podcast. When not writing or editing he can be found behind the desk at the Beaverton City Library, where he finds much inspiration.

Kate Wylie

Kate Wylie (she/they) is a poet from St. Louis, Missouri. An MFA candidate at Pacific University and 2018 Webster University alum, Wylie reads fiction for *The New Southern Fugitives* and is a regular contributor to the Ehlers-Danlos Syndrome society magazine *Loose Connections*.

Nicholas Yandell

Nicholas Yandell is a composer, who sometimes creates with words instead of sound. In those cases, he usually ends up with fiction and occasionally poetry. He also paints and draws, and often all these activities become combined, because they're really not all that different from each other, and it's all just art right?

When not working on creative projects, Nick works as a bookseller at Powell's Books in Portland, Oregon, where he enjoys being surrounded by a wealth of knowledge, as well as working and interacting with creatively stimulating people. He has a website where he displays his creations; it's nicholasyandell.com. Check it out!

Yuanbing Zhang

Yuanbing Zhang (b. 1974), who is a Chinese poet and translator, works in a Middle School, Yanzhou District, Jining City, Shandong Province, China.

All rights to the works contained in this journal belong to their respective authors. Any ideas or beliefs presented by these authors do not necessarily reflect the ideas or beliefs held by Deep Overstock's *editors.*

CPSIA information can be obtained
at www.ICGtesting.com
Printed in the USA
FSHW011736080721
83026FS